BELIEVER

DOVE SEASON

ROBIN BRANDE

RYER PUBLISHING

BELIEVER
(Dove Season)
By Robin Brande

Published by Ryer Publishing
www.ryerpublishing.com
Copyright 2025 by Robin Brande
www.robinbrande.com
Cover art by Anton Chechotkin/Deposit Photos
Cover design by Ryer Publishing
All rights reserved.
Print ISBN: 978-1-952383-28-1
Ebook ISBN: 978-1-952383-13-7

ALSO BY ROBIN BRANDE

<u>Dove Season Universe</u>

Dove Season

Finder

Seeker

Believer

Maker

Explorer

<u>Winnie Parsons Mysteries</u>

The Genius Track

A Man of Appetites

A Drop of Sweat

The Long Gray Hook

The Slip of a Rib

<u>Parallelogram Quartet</u>

Into the Parallel

Caught in the Parallel

Seize the Parallel

Beyond the Parallel

<u>Young Adult</u>

Evolution, Me & Other Freaks of Nature

Fat Cat

Doggirl

Replay

<u>Bradamante Saga</u>

Book of Earth

Book of Water

<u>Romance</u>

Love Proof

Freefall

Heart of Ice

Fire and Ice

<u>Collections</u>

The Love of a Good Dog

Mountain Tough

The Miraculous Unknown

<u>Self-Help</u>

What If You're Doing It Right?

What If You're Doing It Right? For Teens

CONTENTS

DOVE SEASON UNIVERSE
RECOMMENDED READING ORDER

Dove Season

Finder

Seeker

Believer

Maker

Explorer

BELIEVER

BEAR CREEK 1972

1

Travis Baird planted another seed in the loose soil of the window box. His wife, Rosie, loved color. This would be a spring ritual now, he hoped for many years, planting red and pink geraniums that would blossom in June when it really did feel like spring in the mountains.

He could hear Rosie and their seven-year-old daughter, Caroline, inside the little cottage where they had moved a few months ago, just before the start of the spring semester at Mountain State College. The two of them were baking a carrot cake for Travis's thirty-third birthday.

A birthday Travis hadn't been certain he would ever live to see.

The position in the biology department at Mountain

State had opened up just in time. Travis was at loose ends. He had already stepped down as a botany professor at Colorado State University in Fort Collins and quit his position on the team of his former mentor, Dr. Alvin Linsk.

What had once been a project lauded and financed by various governmental and military entities had fallen out of favor in the last year or two. Now there were spies all over the biology department, from the secretarial staff to other professors, all of them looking for ways to discredit whatever findings Linsk's team of scientists made.

Findings about the existence and movements of alien life forms on Earth. Travis's territory had been the Four Corners area of the U.S.: Arizona, New Mexico, Colorado, and Utah. Dr. Linsk's team members were usually the first ones on site whenever there were reports of UFOs or other unexplained phenomena in the area.

Over the eight years Travis had been working for Dr. Linsk, he had identified six different species of aliens. Two of them were highly dangerous and aggressive, but the rest seemed reasonably passive. It was hard to know how long each of the species had been here. Some might have only begun arriving in the past decade or so, others might have infiltrated the planet long ago.

That had been part of the overall project, not only

identifying them biologically, but also trying to determine their origins and history.

But Travis was off the team for good now. Even though when he first quit, Dr. Linsk begged him to stay.

There were other scientists still working out in the field, still doing the important investigations. They interviewed witnesses to suspected extraterrestrial visitations, they gathered samples from the area, they took measurements and tested the radiation levels around where alien craft had landed.

But there was a cost to that knowledge. Travis and the other investigators grew sick with mysterious illnesses. It might have been because of the radiation, or it could be because the biological remnants of the aliens' presence attacked the human body in unexpected ways.

Whatever the reason, the field agents had suspiciously short life spans.

Travis himself had been visibly weakening and wasting away for the past few years, suffering from a series of devastating ailments.

He treasured every moment he could spend with Rosie and Caroline. He expected those moments were rapidly dwindling down.

Until last September.

Travis followed a lead to a different kind of alien. A species he had heard rumors of, but had never encountered himself.

He read a report of man who had been abducted in a

farmer's field in a place called Red Rock, about thirty miles northwest of Tucson, Arizona.

Travis had seen the man with his own eyes. A hale and hearty middle-aged farm hand named Raoul Ortega.

A man who had been dying of cancer until the aliens took him.

The aliens were a species people were calling the Healers. They had to be. Travis hoped to God they were.

He drove out to Tucson on his own, without Dr. Linsk's or anyone else's authority, hoping to find where the aliens were.

Hoping from the bottom of his soul that they might be able to heal him, too.

He didn't tell Rosie. He didn't want to get her hopes up. He didn't tell his boss or anyone else.

But from the moment he walked out across the moonlit field where Mr. Ortega had been abducted, and saw ahead of him the alien coming to meet him, Travis knew.

He had already seen and learned things in the past eight years that defied his assumptions about biological science and the Earth and the nature of the greater universe.

But this was about to be an experience that surpassed all the others.

His escort, a woman named Mercedes Fuentes, had

the ability to communicate with the alien Healers. She had been speaking to them telepathically for years.

She brought Travis to them and made some kind of telepathic introduction. Then Mercedes Fuentes left and Travis followed the alien life form back to her ship.

There were two aliens that night, both of them humanoid in appearance. Actually, although he hadn't told Rosie this yet, they looked like beautiful human women. The most beautiful women he had ever seen.

Like a mermaid, Travis had heard Raoul Ortega describe the one who picked him up in her arms and carried him after he collapsed. She had webbed fingers and toes and long silvery hair and large silvery blue eyes.

Travis had no need of a flashlight as he followed her across the nighttime field. Her body glowed like a bioluminescent sea creature. He could have read a newspaper by the light of her silvery skin.

She wore no clothes that he could see, although he realized later that her body was wrapped tightly in some kind of suit that acted as a second skin. It was the suit that was silver. Her true skin was a light pale green. And it was that skin that glowed so beautifully. He could see it coming through more clearly in her uncovered face and hands.

Travis couldn't stop staring at her. He walked beside her, not paying attention to his feet, but he felt like he was gliding, just as she was, across the rough surface of the clod-covered field.

Her face was more beautiful than a movie star's. It was … perfection. Everything about her seemed graceful and feminine and exquisite. But she wasn't the kind of woman a man would lust after. She was too angelic and pure for that.

And what was there to lust after? The alien had no outward feminine shape to draw the eye. No breasts, no indication of her sex at all. But her long silver hair and her flawless face still made him feel sure that the creature was a woman.

And when she spoke to him, he knew it for certain.

"Are you afraid?" she asked Travis in a soft and lilting voice that was as lovely and feminine as her face.

He didn't answer right away. He wanted to tell the truth, and the truth was he wasn't sure how he felt.

Elated. That was the word for it.

"No," he told her, "I'm not afraid."

She reached down with her warm, webbed fingers and clasped Travis's hand.

He could feel warmth spreading up his arm and all through his body. Like the feeling of slipping into a slightly warm bath. Not too hot, not something to make you suck in your breath and ease slowly until you got used to it. The warmth felt instantly comfortable—and comforting. Travis could feel a sob want to loosen from his chest.

A memory flashed into his mind. He didn't know if it was a real memory, or more of an association.

He could see himself, feel himself, as a tiny boy, barely older than a baby. He felt his mother's arms scoop him up out of a cold cradle and hug him into her warm chest.

He imagined he could feel her heartbeat, steady, reassuring. He felt so safe. So loved. So cared for. Whatever childhood nightmare had woken him up screaming and crying for help was now gone in an instant.

He felt that way now, as if all of the fear and worry of the past few years simply misted away from his mind. He didn't have to hold so hard to the idea of wanting to stay alive to see Rosie and Caroline. He wasn't afraid anymore of dying and being alone.

Up ahead he could see a shape in the dark. There was no color or reflection that his eyes could see, just a change to the uniform blackness.

"Will you come with us?" the beautiful alien asked him.

Travis hesitated again. "For how long?"

The woman turned to him and favored him with her calm, angelic smile.

"Not long," she said. "We will help you."

Travis couldn't imagine telling her no.

He nodded and the alien swept her right arm through the dark, and a light came from the shape in front of them.

Travis could see the outline of a ship now, like two clamshells placed together, broad enough at its center that the alien at his side could easily stand at her full height.

At the center, at the widest part, there was a round door shaped like an open mouth.

The light was coming from there. Visible from inside the craft.

He could see the second alien now, standing in the round doorway, smiling in the same pure and angelic way.

She, too, had long silvery hair that reached down to her waist, and the same oddly-shaped eyes, like ovals lying on their sides, and twice the size of a human's.

Travis paused. He could feel his heart racing. If they were going to kill him…

But they had healed Raoul Ortega. They had abducted him and brought him back healed.

Travis said a prayer he remembered from his childhood. Only the line that seemed made for an occasion like this. *Yea, though I walk through the Valley of the Shadow of Death, I shall fear no evil…*

He didn't believe these aliens were evil. He … hoped they weren't.

He took a step forward, and then another.

He stepped through the open mouth of the spaceship, and it swallowed him inside.

2

"You have to make a wish," Caroline told him, just as Travis was about to blow out his candles.

"Oh, I forgot," he said. "Okay, hold on." He shut his eyes tightly.

He already had everything he wished for.

Asking for anything more felt greedy.

But Caroline was right. A birthday wish had to be made. Otherwise it was bad luck.

Travis thought the wish privately to himself. Then he opened his eyes and blew out thirty-three white candles. Rosie and Caroline clapped.

They sat in the cozy little kitchen of their cottage. Rosie had painted the dull ivory walls a bright cheerful yellow right after they moved in. She sewed pink gingham curtains for the window and made a matching table cloth for their small round oak table they brought from the other house.

They hadn't brought very much. Just two beds, two dressers, the kitchen table and three chairs, and a light blue sofa and matching upholstered chair that Rosie's parents had given them as a hand-me-down when they first got married.

Travis always planned on buying new furniture some day when he was finally earning enough. But that day never seemed to come.

And now he was working for even less than before.

But it was worth it. He and Rosie both knew it. They couldn't stay in Fort Collins. Not after what happened. And not with all the turmoil in the biology department.

Decisions had to be made, and Travis and Rosie made them. No looking back. Only forward. They were in this together. Their family was all that mattered.

Dr. Linsk had been willing to help them. He made excuses for why Travis remained out in the field for another few months and never returned to his lab or his office in the biology department.

They continued trying to communicate on phone calls, but after a few times of hearing clicks on the line, Travis was too paranoid to continue.

They met once in a neighborhood park on the edge of town.

Dr. Linsk's expression told Travis all he needed to know.

Of course Travis had changed. Of course anyone with eyes would be able to see it.

He had regained the twenty pounds that he had watched slough off his frame. His thinning, graying hair was now its former thick brown. The lines and creases on his face had practically disappeared. Travis looked twenty-five again. Rosie swore it.

There was a vigor to his step that he hadn't felt in years. Until September he had been walking with a stoop, like an arthritic old man.

Linsk whispered, "Good God," and he swiped his hand over his brow. He took out his handkerchief and mopped the sweat from above his lip.

"So you see why I have to go," Travis said.

Dr. Linsk nodded mutely. There was no question anymore.

They sat at a picnic table under the yellowing autumn leaves of a stand of aspens. Dr. Linsk drew out his pipe and tobacco pouch from the pockets of his brown wool sports coat and took his time filling and tamping the pipe bowl and then lighting it and puffing. Travis was familiar with the technique. Alvin Linsk's way of stalling, of buying himself time to think before he was ready to speak.

Travis breathed in the woodsy smell of the tobacco as he studied his old boss. Alvin Linsk had noticeably aged in the eight years they had worked together. The top of his head was almost completely bald now. He wore thicker lenses in his black horn rim glasses. His belly had filled out, and now sloped over the top of his trousers. He looked careworn. Travis could understand that. Until a month ago, he had looked halfway to death himself.

But despite all the current turmoil in the biology department and on the investigative team, Alvin Linsk was still Travis's friend and mentor. And he had university contacts all over the country. There had to be another job somewhere that Travis could take to support his family.

A job out of the public eye. Something low key. Someplace where Travis could detach himself from the work he had done for the military and the government. Just another field agent, no one special, just burned out on the work and looking for something easier.

There might have been places further away, but Rosie asked that they stay at least somewhat close to her parents. Travis agreed. They were Caroline's only grandparents now. There would be enough change without tearing her away from them.

So when the job opening came up in December at Mountain State College in the small mountain town of Bear Creek, Colorado, Travis threw his heart into trying to win the position. Dr. Linsk had nothing to do with it, other than giving Travis a glowing recommendation. But he didn't know anyone at the college or anyone in Bear Creek.

That was fine with Travis. He wanted as few ties to the past as possible. He needed a clean break. Bear Creek was it.

Some other scientist with Travis's credentials and years of experience might think it was a step down to go back to teaching basic biology to freshmen, and at a school much less prestigious than Colorado State University. But Travis's enthusiasm during his interview was sincere, and it obviously convinced the head of the biology department that he'd found his man.

With the new job assured, Travis stayed a few extra hours before driving back home to look around for a place to rent that he could afford on their new budget.

A secretary at the college directed him to these cottages. She said a lot of the younger faculty rented them until they could afford a bigger place.

It was a step down and Travis knew it, but Rosie acted as if it was just a notch shy of a palace.

When he brought her to see it she gripped Travis's hand and told him, "It's perfect." Then she set out to make it as pretty as possible.

And after the first month, when they realized Travis's salary still wouldn't meet all their bills, Rosie took a typing job at the college, working for a history professor who was writing a book. The cottage was close enough to Caroline's school that she could walk or ride her bike, and it was on the bus line to campus so Travis and Rosie could ride into work together.

Everything had come together so much more smoothly than Travis had imagined.

And now he was celebrating a birthday he had never been guaranteed to have. It was a beautiful Sunday afternoon. There were still patches of snow on the ground, but the birds were singing lustily in the trees.

Travis felt happier and more peaceful than any birthday in recent memory.

And then came the knock on the door.

Not a knock, more of a pounding. *Bam, bam, bam,* from a heavy fist. Caroline's friends from school sometimes came over to ask her to play, but this wasn't the sound of a seven-year-old's knuckles on the door.

Travis froze. He looked at Rosie. Her eyes were wide and frightened. Caroline was busy pulling the birthday candles out of the cake, and didn't notice her parents' reaction.

"I'll get it!" she sang as she jumped up from her chair.

But Rosie quickly grabbed her thin arm. "No, honey, let Daddy get it."

The kitchen had only one window, and it looked out over the small back yard.

Travis motioned for Rosie and Caroline to stay behind. He strode swiftly and as quietly as he could toward the living room window.

He gazed out through the sliver between the ruffled curtain and the window frame.

There was a dark sedan parked in front of the cottage. He didn't recognize it.

Bam, bam, bam. Whoever was out there was getting impatient.

Travis went to the door. He didn't know what to expect when he opened it. But he had been afraid of a visitation ever since he left Fort Collins.

At the end of his meeting in the park with Dr. Linsk, Travis had asked what he should with all his extensive notebooks filled during his years of investigations.

All of the investigators turned in regular monthly reports with details taken from their raw notes. But all of them kept their notebooks for themselves. Dr. Linsk wanted the notes kept separate as both an extra copy and as proof in case some of the reports were ever altered in any way.

In the beginning Travis thought it seemed like an unnecessary precaution, but over time he came to see it as essential.

Reports were, in fact, altered. More and more frequently over the years. Some of the changes were so laughably obvious, Travis couldn't believe whoever made them thought they could get away with it.

But they did get away with it. And then the work as a whole was so much more easily discredited.

As far as the greater public knew, every single UFO sighting had been debunked. There were no aliens. All of it had been a big hoax.

But Travis still had proof. It was there in eight years of his field notebooks. He had never wondered what to do with them before, but now he was leaving.

Technically, they might belong to the people who had funded Travis's work. Whether it was Colorado State University, or the military, or the government.

But Travis had visions of his notebooks being ripped to shreds, or thrown into a pile and burned.

He had his own ideas about what he should do with his field notes. But he wanted Linsk's opinion first.

"Honestly?" Dr. Linsk told him. "Keep them. Hide them."

It was exactly what Travis wanted to do.

And now the visitation had come. Travis opened the door. Dr. Alvin Linsk stood on the concrete doorstep looking white-faced and nervous.

Accompanied by two men in dark suits, to match the dark sedan.

Government men. Agents. Travis knew the look. He had met more than a few of them over the past eight years.

Sometimes they came out to the sites where Travis was investigating and took away artifacts before he had the chance to secure them.

He had once wrestled with a man in a dark suit and dark sunglasses who tried to steal a carved figurine Travis found near a reported landing site of a UFO.

But he was much younger then, and as the field work

took its toll, Travis gave up trying to match any of the dark suits' muscle.

These men were typical. Broad-shouldered and tough-looking. They stared at Travis with grim expressions.

"Happy Birthday," said Dr. Linsk, as if that was why they came.

Then the dark suit on Linsk's left shouldered his way into the house, and Dr. Linsk and the other dark suit followed.

"Come on in," Travis said, as if they had waited for his invitation. But he was determined to be polite to his old boss Linsk, if not to the other two.

Travis's heart was hammering. It would do no good to show fear. He had to play this off. He had to act as though he had nothing to hide.

"These gentleman would like to take a look around," said Dr. Linsk.

"I'd rather they didn't," Travis answered.

"I know," Linsk said, "but I'm afraid they have to."

"National Secrets Act," said the brawnier of the two suits. "We have reason to believe you stole government property."

"Travis?" Rosie said quietly. She and Caroline were standing at the door of the kitchen. Caroline looked afraid and hid behind Rosie's hip, but Rosie was trying to appear calm.

"It's all right," Travis said. "Why don't you two go on outside? This will only take a few minutes."

Travis mouthed, *"Go,"* and Rosie went. They had talked about this before. She exited through the back door and then kept on walking.

Travis waited until he thought they had enough time to pass through the back gate and out of the yard. He realized too late they hadn't had time to grab coats before they left. But he knew Rosie would find someplace warm for the two of them to wait. Maybe at the coffee shop up the street. Travis didn't need to worry about the girls.

He had enough worries as it was. He turned back to his visitors and let out a sigh.

"Okay, boys," he said, "what is this? What exactly do you want?"

Dr. Linsk was still trying to sound diplomatic. Ever the gracious host to the people who were still paying his department at least a hundred thousand dollars a year to draw up plans for a biodome on the moon in case humanity ever wanted to live there.

"It seems I forgot to report to them that you quit," said Dr. Linsk. "I was supposed to collect a few things from you before you left."

"Hold on," Travis said. He had planned this, too. He went to his bedroom and rooted around in the top drawer of his dresser.

He didn't have an office at home. No desk or filing

cabinets. Just the few pieces of furniture in the cottage's few rooms.

He brought back a slim black leather wallet and handed it to the less brawny of the two agents. The man flipped it open. Travis's identification was inside.

It was the government-issued identification that he flashed if anyone questioned his authority to be in places he needed to see.

"I'm sorry," he told Dr. Linsk. "I should have mailed it to you. I'm sorry you fellows had to come all the way out here."

"We're here for the notebooks," the beefier agent said. "But I'm sure you know that, Dr. Baird."

"The ... notebooks?" Travis repeated, trying to sound genuinely confused.

"Your field notes," said Dr. Linsk.

Travis scoffed. "You won't be able to read them. I can barely read my handwriting myself. I put all those things in my monthly reports. Don't you still have those?"

"The notebooks, Dr. Baird," said the large and in charge agent.

Travis sighed again. "All right," he said, still sounding skeptical. "But it's going to be like reading hiero-glyphics."

He could feel his right hand shaking with nerves. He steadied it against his thigh.

He had thought about a day like this so many times in the past few months. He always hoped he was letting his imagination run away with him. But now he was glad for every single step of preparation he had made.

He went back to his bedroom and opened the closet door. There was barely room in there for even the few clothes he and Rosie brought from their other life.

He kept the notebooks in a ratty-looking cardboard moving box. He hoped it showed that he didn't consider them important anymore. They weren't displayed out in the living room on the small set of shelves he had built out of bricks and boards. He pulled out a spare blanket from the top of the box and then lifted out the books in two separate stacks.

The style of them varied. Some had hard cardboard covers, others had more supple leather. Travis thumbed through the one on top to show Linsk, knowing the agents were looking over his shoulder.

"I mean, look at this," Travis said. "You can't even read them."

But his heart sped as the pages flipped by showing his detailed drawings from every investigation. Some were renditions of descriptions he got from witnesses. Some were his own sketches of evidence he found at the scenes.

The lesser agent reached past Linsk and snatched the notebook out of Travis's hand. "The rest of them, Dr. Baird," he said. Travis felt sick with regret as he handed the precious notebooks over.

He had done his best to preserve his work of the past

eight years. But nothing would replace his original drawings, in particular. It was like handing over valuable works of art to gorillas he knew would just smash them and rip them up.

Travis felt tired suddenly. He wanted these men to go. Alvin Linsk, too. All of them.

"Is that all?" Travis asked.

Linsk grunted as he stood back up. "It is. Sorry to trouble you, especially on your birthday. My love to the girls."

Travis nodded and mumbled *uh-huh*.

He did not bother getting up and seeing the men out. He thought it would seem more realistic for him to stay behind, obviously upset.

It was no act. But Travis knew it would have been so immensely worse if he hadn't prepared for it as best as he could.

He locked the door behind the three visitors and watched out the living room window as they drove away.

He wondered if he would ever see his old boss again. He didn't mind it if he didn't.

Linsk was just doing what he had to, but Travis couldn't help wondering whether his former friend and mentor put up any kind of fight at all.

Dr. Linsk was still in charge of an entire biology department and looked forward to the money he got from his masters to continue keeping the whole ship afloat.

Travis put the spare blanket back in the moving box and pushed it back into the corner of the closet. He shut the door and walked back to the kitchen to wait for Rosie and Caroline's return.

From his vantage on the spindle-backed oak chair, he looked around at the bright yellow kitchen. He tried to see it through Linsk's and the two agents' eyes. It must have looked quaint and harmless and unimportant.

Travis moved to the doorway of the kitchen and looked across at the small living room at the front of the house. He conducted the same objective observation. What did those men see when they barged their way into the cottage?

They saw a poor college professor who was even poorer than before. There was nothing special about Travis Baird.

Travis could finally smile to himself about that.

Rosie had worked very hard for the past three months, typing before the history professor came into work, and then typing over all of her lunch hours.

They discussed whether it was honest, especially to use the college's typing supplies. But they agreed that the need was too great to worry about small ethical issues right now. They needed to preserve Travis's notes.

One by one, Rosie brought the notebooks to work with her and spent hours deciphering her husband's poor penmanship. But Rosie could read Travis's scrawls, whereas some other typist would have been lost.

When she finished one notebook she brought it home and took up another. They were careful that there would always be a stack of notebooks in the moving box, in case people came to grab them some day like today.

There was still a notebook in the history department right now, in a drawer of the desk where Rosie sat.

She had already finished typing it—it was the last one—but she couldn't bear to let all of Travis's work go. She convinced him they should keep it. Proof, she said, of the man her husband was. Smart, thorough, imaginative, brave—she wanted to make sure that Caroline could see it for herself some day.

When Rosie finished typing each of the notebooks, she punched the typewritten pages with a three-hole punch and brought them home in a canvas satchel she dedicated to just this work. And then she and Travis divided the pages among various locations throughout the cottage, each of the pages carefully dated and numbered so they could be assembled in their correct order again some day.

Some were in the three-ring binder of recipes Rosie had copied down from her mother's collection. The notebook sat on the counter next to the toaster, visible for anyone to see.

But the two brawny agents wouldn't have given even

a moment's attention to a homemaker's recipe book. Travis and Rosie counted on it. It had been Rosie's idea.

She also suggested filling up some of Caroline's notebooks from school. There was a three-ring binder in Caroline's room that had a green corduroy cover. Caroline had drawn a bird and flower on it with a black Magic Marker. There was also one with a cover made out of denim with a pocket on front to make it look like a pair of jeans. They had filled that one, too. But no one would give a second look to a seven-year-old's school books.

There were several three-ring photo albums on the shelves in the living room, and Travis's field notes were interspersed among pages of photographs of the family.

And Rosie had made several fabric covers for plain three-ring notebooks and written in her lovely cursive on the spines titles like Bible Stories and Fairy Tales and Favorite Childhood Fables.

Every single one of Travis's notebooks was contained within the little cottage.

The words were there, preserved on typewritten pages, but the drawings had been much harder to duplicate.

Travis borrowed graph paper from the math department at the college and spent every night and the weekends copying what he had drawn in the field.

Those drawings were lying flat in a stack and folded inside the spare blanket currently in the ratty-looking moving box on the floor of Travis's closet. That was Rosie's idea, too. She doubted anyone would open the old blanket. People felt strange handling other people's bedwear.

And then there was the gift.

Travis had never told Alvin Linsk about that.

He had given him a rendition of the experience with the two beautiful aliens, but Travis had deliberately kept some of the details for himself.

Nobody except Travis and Rosie knew about the gift the aliens had given him.

A strange metal instrument, dull gray and shaped like a pistol, but without any other features of an Earth-based gun. No trigger, no openings anywhere, just a piece of lightweight, unearthly metal bent at a ninety-degree angle.

It responded to the user's touch, the alien he knew as Quella had told him after their night was done. The other alien, Rill, was busy setting their spaceship back down on the farmer's fallow field.

It was a healing torch, as far as he understood the image and words Quella was putting inside his head. A way to heal himself if ever needed it again, and to heal the people he loved.

The artifact was currently buried at the bottom of a large flower pot sitting outside the kitchen door. Rosie had wrapped it carefully in an empty bread bag, then they both covered it with clean dirt. Rosie said she might plant petunias there in the summer, although Travis wasn't sure that was wise. The artifact looked impermeable to water, but he didn't dare risk harming it in any way.

He hadn't made a drawing of the artifact in his field book. He had left out a variety of different details. He knew by the time he wrote in his book that he wouldn't be transcribing it into any report later.

He already knew he couldn't go back to the investigative team. He looked and felt too different.

It was time to move on. Even though he had no idea where he would go or what he would do. But his night with the aliens had changed him too profoundly to resume his previous life and pretend nothing had happened.

He tried to sketch the two aliens' beautiful faces, but his skills were too crude to do them justice. Maybe only Michelangelo could capture how divine the two of them looked. Travis looked at what he drew and almost ripped it out of his book. He might as well have drawn them as stick figures, for all that his scratches on the page had conveyed what his eyes beheld.

He drew their smaller spaceship that he saw out on the field, but he didn't draw the larger ship where they took him. He wasn't sure why. Somehow it felt too private. But whatever the reason, he obeyed his instinct.

The larger ship wasn't much larger than a commercial airplane. It was completely round, disk-shaped, like so many of the other UFOs witnesses had described to Travis over the years.

If there were other aliens on board it, Travis never saw them. He remained with only Quella and Rill.

There was only one compartment that he ever saw in the larger ship. He felt he was standing in a round room the size of his entire house back in Fort Collins.

There were lights shining softly from somewhere out of the ceiling. There was a platform in the center of the room, floating above the floor at about the height of Travis's waist. The platform was about as wide as a twin bed, but longer, long enough for someone very tall to lie on top of it.

That was what Quella wanted from him next: to lie down on top of the platform. Travis felt no fear. He was there to be healed, and the platform seemed like the kind of examining table he might find at a doctor's office.

He stretched out on his back and noticed how soft and pliable the platform felt. Not as soft as a pillow or a mattress, but still very comfortable against his bones.

Quella took up her position to the right of Travis's head. The other alien, Rill, stood at her side, ready to assist the way a nurse would assist a surgeon.

Rill handed Quella a series of colored, glowing rods the size and shape of tapered candles.

Quella directed the tips of the glowing rods at various spots on Travis's body. The lights emanating from them were beautiful. Soft, never too bright for his eyes, in colors of green and yellow and blue.

Travis thought he could feel the cells in his body respond, although it might have only been his imagination.

But he felt safe. He knew that they were trying to help him. Not only trying—he believed they could do it.

When the work was done and Quella returned the last of the glowing rods to Rill, she helped Travis sit up on the platform. He dangled his legs over the side. He could feel a gentle buzzing from his calves to his toes. He felt slightly light-headed at first, but then all the strange sensations passed. And Travis knew without a doubt he was entirely healed.

Tears welled in his eyes. He tried to find the words to tell the two aliens how grateful he was.

Then Rill handed Quella one more instrument, and Quella held it up for Travis to inspect.

It was another small metal rod, but this one was thinner and dull gray and about the size of a pencil. It had a small flat tip on one end, like a miniature spatula.

Quella asked some equivalent of, "May I?" Travis couldn't remember the exact words, but he remembered the feeling of her asking for his permission.

He didn't know what she wanted, but he nodded nevertheless. How could he refuse her anything now?

She opened her mouth wide to demonstrate that Travis should do the same. Once he did, she angled the metal rod inside and he could feel the flat tip scraping against the inside of his cheek.

Rill was standing by with a small spherical receptacle. It was about the size of a tennis ball, and glowed with a faint bluish light. Quella slipped the flat tip of the rod into a hole in the top of the sphere. Once she removed the instrument, the hole closed up on its own.

In his field notes Travis wrote about the procedure in his mouth, and he drew the rod with the flat tip and the glowing sphere. He wrote that he thought they might have taken a sample of his cells, but that he was only speculating. Quella never told him what it was for.

He also wrote down the directions of where Quella and Rill seemed to indicate they came from. What sounded like a warm rocky planet in the Pleiades cluster of stars.

Travis tried to remember as many details as he could the next morning after they left him in the field. He walked to where Mercedes Fuentes had promised to meet him with his car.

She greeted him with a smile almost as angelic as the aliens'. "You are well," she said, beaming. "I knew."

Travis asked her to drive so he could sit in the passenger seat and write. Mercedes piloted the Plymouth back along the dusty farm roads out to the highway and back to Tucson.

She parked outside her shop where she sold gifts and clothing imported from Mexico. But Travis knew the shop was merely a front for the more important work Mercedes Fuentes did. She, too, investigated extraterrestrial sightings all across the world.

But she had an advantage that Travis and the other investigators didn't have. She could communicate with some of the aliens telepathically.

"May I see this?" she asked him, reaching gently for the gift he had kept on his lap throughout the journey.

Mercedes turned the artifact in her hands, examining it this way and that. Then she returned it to Travis's keeping.

"They do not give lightly," Mercedes said. "This is the first time that I've heard of. You must understand what an honor this is."

"But why did they give it to me?" Travis asked her. "I'm nobody special. Why me?"

Mercedes closed her eyes. Travis wondered if she was communicating with Quella or Rill, but the moment was brief. Maybe Mercedes was just carefully choosing how much to tell him.

"Time is different for them," said Mercedes. "They are not stopped in the present like you and me."

"Are you saying they can see the future?" Travis asked.

Mercedes nodded. "They have never told me, but that is what I think."

"So they gave this to me ... why?" Travis asked again. "Do you think they see some future when I use it?"

"I am sure you will use it," she said. "They would not give it to you for nothing." Mercedes shrugged. "But who can say?"

Travis thanked her for her help. It was Mercedes who had made the connection for Travis, first with Raoul Ortega, and then with the beautiful aliens.

If not for her, he might be driving back to Fort Collins and his wife and child, still desperately ill, still on the rapidly accelerating road to death.

"*De nada*," Mercedes said. She leaned across the seat and kissed Travis on the cheek. Then she opened the door and got out of the car.

Travis watched her unlock her shop. She paused at the door and waved before disappearing inside. He wondered if he would ever see her again. He thought not. He thought his days of chasing aliens were probably over.

He wanted a simple life. A safe and quiet life. Quella and Rill had given him a second chance. Travis was ready to start over.

And it meant disentangling himself from the secret work he had been doing for the military and the government. He needed to be free of them. Whatever they were doing, they would have to do it without him.

Travis still felt that way now, sitting in the little yellow kitchen of his cottage. Rosie and Caroline had returned within the hour and resumed his birthday celebration.

Caroline didn't seem plagued by any lingering fears about the visit from the agents. Travis was glad of it. She was a cheerful, inquisitive child, and he wanted her always to feel safe.

That night, when Rosie joined him in bed, Travis held her close and breathed in the peach scent of her freshly washed hair.

"Is it over?" Rosie asked. "Are they ever coming back?"

"I think it's over," Travis said.

But as he lay awake on his thirty-third birthday, with his wife nestled warmly in his arms, Travis mulled over the events of the afternoon, from the bang on his door to the agents driving away.

He still burned at the thought of his notebooks and all their uniquely valuable information now being in the hands of those government thugs.

They had probably destroyed them by now. And Alvin Linsk had probably stood by and watched them do it.

It was the way of the world now, and Travis couldn't do anything about it.

He and Rosie had done the best that they could to preserve what they did. He had to be satisfied with that.

But he couldn't help wishing he had handled things differently all along. He might have kept a separate set of notebooks just for himself. He could have done his drawings in those and never shown them to anyone else.

He didn't have to send in such meticulous monthly reports. He thought he was doing something important. He sweated over every detail of his work.

But what did any of that work matter now? It was all being discredited. The public was never going to hear the truth.

But the fact was, the work did matter. It still did. Even though Travis wasn't investigating them anymore, he knew there must be just as many sightings of UFOs now as there were over the past eight years.

He hoped that some of his old colleagues were still going out there to do the work. It couldn't stop just because pursuing the truth had become unpopular.

Travis's mind drifted then, as it often did these days, to his last conversation with Mercedes Fuentes.

About how the two of them were stopped in the present, but the alien healers could see into the future.

What did they see, Quella and Rill, when they looked into Travis's future? Not only his, but the whole of the human race's?

Why had they given him the secret gift he kept hidden in the flower pot in his back yard? Mercedes said it was an honor. *They do not give lightly.* If so, why had they chosen Travis to receive such a gift? What did they intend for him to do with it?

He felt a nagging idea. Brought on by the events of the day. If the alien healers had seen this day in the future ... was this the reason why?

Travis's original notebooks were gone. His proof of everything he had learned and seen. The typewritten copies were important, but they weren't the same.

The ink wasn't smudged with Travis's sweat. The pages weren't dusted with dirt from the field. Those notebooks were artifacts, just like the gift that Quella had given to Travis.

All of them were proof that aliens existed.

They not only existed, they were here. Here on Earth.

Wasn't that the point of Travis's work? To prove that?

Travis carefully removed his arm from behind Rosie's head. Rosie gently stirred, but continued sleeping.

Travis padded barefooted out to the living room. He kept his briefcase set next to the door. There were notes in there of the topics he wanted to cover in his upcoming lectures. And there were plenty of blank sheets of notebook paper for his future ideas.

He could buy a more formal notebook on campus tomorrow between classes. But for right now, he just needed to start putting some of his thoughts on paper.

He took the stack of blank pages with him into the kitchen.

Dr. Travis Baird sat at the table and began to write.

DIVISION

1

Maybe some people could forget what they saw. Unknow what they knew. But Gina Firenzi couldn't.

One month ago, on New Year's Day, she knew that the man crowding behind her down a narrow hallway in a rundown, disgusting house was not a real cop, despite what he pretended.

More important, Gina knew—she *felt* it—that the man was going to kill her. He was going to shoot her in the back. And not only shoot her, but also Mrs. Byers, the elegant, white-haired old lady Gina had brought along to assist on the case she was investigating.

It was a split-second decision, but Gina knew it was the right one. She didn't hesitate. She couldn't afford to.

She had smuggled a rusty hunting knife up her sleeve

—part of the strange collection of artifacts she found among her suspect's possessions—and when she could feel the fake cop behind her moving, when she knew he had pulled his gun and was about to use it, Gina spun around and shoved the knife in his chest. He fought back, but Gina fought too. At five-foot-eleven she had some mass to bring to bear.

They fought and Gina won. She got Mrs. Byers out of that squalid house before any of the fake cop's accomplices could show up to finish what he didn't.

And she managed to smuggle out one more strange artifact from the suspect's collection: a small leather bound notebook completely filled with what Gina at first thought were illegible scribblings, but that turned out to be the kind of indecipherable symbols only a cryptologist could appreciate.

She had turned it over to one of her colleagues at the Agency who specialized in decoding pictographs like that. So far, no progress. Not even a single word deciphered.

But Gina had other problems.

Primarily, what to do with this new truth she had stumbled on and simply couldn't ignore. She was an investigator. Not only by profession, but by inclination. Maybe someone else could set aside what had happened, could compartmentalize it and decide it belonged in the realm of *Other*, and there were plenty of things to work on without ever thinking about it or going near it again

—but that wasn't Gina. She had to know. She had to dig deeper.

And that had become the problem.

Gina had been an investigator with the Agency for the past ten years. She loved the work. It was both a physical and mental challenge. She loved being in the field. Other investigators who came in when she did were already supervisors and heads of divisions. Gina wasn't interested in managing other agents. She wanted to get her hands dirty and solve cases for herself.

But a door had opened on New Year's Day, and Gina didn't want to close it.

She knew what happened in that hallway. Whether someone would call it intuition or extrasensory or even just luck—Gina had gotten a clear, unmistakable message from somewhere other than her logical brain, and it told her *Danger. Move. NOW.*

If she had ignored it, questioned it, dismissed it—

But she didn't. It was the only reason she was still here. And even if a thousand different experts wanted to tell her she was crazy to think there was anything really to it, Gina didn't care. She knew what she knew what she knew.

The thing was, she wasn't the first at the Agency to want to investigate forces beyond what her five senses could reveal. For twenty years, most of it before her time, there had been a division of the Agency that used what they called Finders. It was a more acceptable term,

Gina assumed, than some others that got thrown around: psychics, sensitives, *freaks.*

Mrs. Byers had been a Finder back in those days. It was why Gina brought her along on her case on New Year's Day. She had only two hours inside a mass shooter's house to look around and see if she could find anything that fit a particular theory Gina was pursuing, and so she wanted to use that brief window as efficiently as possible.

Mrs. Byers could sit inside a building, close her eyes, and poke around psychically from room to room to find what was hidden from investigators' eyes. When Gina found out about the old Finders division, she recruited Mrs. Byers to help her find a stash of files and photographs inside a warehouse that Gina had already searched numerous times without any success.

Mrs. Byers felt around the nooks of the warehouse with her mind, and had Gina's evidence in less than an hour.

So it made sense to ask Mrs. Byers to help her on this second case, and help Gina search the killer's home in the short time they could get in there.

Mrs. Byers closed her eyes and surveyed the whole garbage-ridden house and found several cameras hidden in various rooms and still recording. She also found the killer's stash of money and drugs and the rusty knife and the notebook full of code. Gina never would have found any of them herself. Once again Mrs. Byers had proven she had a special gift.

But now Gina thought she might have one too. At least under pressure, even if it was only some evolutionary special intuition that she used to save their lives.

But it was real. And Gina couldn't just tuck away the memory of it and go about her regular life. She needed to know more. She needed to know all of it.

She had already pulled as many files as she could find about the old Finders division back when she first approached Mrs. Byers about the first case. The last director of the Agency before the current one had shut down the division for whatever reason. Maybe it wasn't politically acceptable anymore. Or probably he thought it was all hooey.

Gina had met the man and never liked him. She was new to the job then, and even though she only spoke with the director a few times, he seemed like the kind of guy who tried to cover his insecurities by acting arrogant and aggressive.

The current Agency director was much more low-key. Not exactly friendly, but that didn't seem to be the job description.

But Gina didn't think her request would have to go up that far. She might be able to handle it more locally, with her own supervisor, Hank Alterra.

Alterra ran his department in an organized but light-handed way. He gave his agents plenty of room to use their talents as suited them best. But he was a good advocate for them with the higher-ups, and acted as a level-headed sounding board when they needed to bounce a theory around or sort through the disjointed facts souping around in their brains.

Not a pushover, but not a tyrant. He was the best boss Gina had ever had.

Every Monday Hank Alterra ran weekly case reviews with all the investigators in the unit, to check their progress and to fill in gaps where other agents could help move a case along.

Gina had waited four weeks to have a certain conversation. She had gathered her facts. Prepared her arguments.

Now was the time.

As the other investigators filed out of the conference room—a glorified name for a tight, windowless room that had only enough space for a long table and a dozen chairs and a small coffee cart in the corner—Gina lingered. Waiting for Hank Alterra to be alone.

He turned from the coffee station where he'd been refilling his to-go cup, and raised an eyebrow when he saw her standing there. He was a handsome man in an old-time adventure movie sort of way, like the guide on a mysterious expedition into the Andes or the jungle. Mid-fifties, rugged, still fit. The desk job hadn't made him soft.

"More?" he asked Gina.

"Just one more thing," she said. She handed him the folder she'd made of all the Finders who were still alive and not only willing, but eager to get back to work.

A lot of the Finders had been old already when the division was at its peak, so some of them had died in the ensuing years.

But besides Mrs. Byers, who was in her seventies, there were five men and four women who still had the skills and the desire to help. All of them were in their sixties and seventies. Gina wouldn't have minded a few closer to her age, in their thirties or forties. But she had to start somewhere. And she wanted to start now.

Hank read the label on Gina's file. "Finders. Wow. Been a while."

"You know I've used Mrs. Byers now a few times."

Hank took a sip of coffee and waited. That was his way. Draw out his agents with silence. Make them do the heavy lifting.

Gina blew out a breath. "So … I think we should take a look at this again. I believe in it. This stuff is real."

"It wasn't too popular," Hank said.

Gina shifted her shoulders back. "Do I care?"

Hank sat back down in the nearest chair. He motioned for Gina to take the seat next to him.

He read through the pages in her file folder while he sipped the Agency's substandard coffee.

Gina used the silence to organize her mind. She

needed to rely on logic, not feelings, if she wanted to convince Alterra to go her way.

"So you want to head this?" Hank asked her.

Gina shrugged. She didn't want to seem too eager. She didn't want her supervisor to ask her too many questions.

She didn't want to have to explain how personal this had all suddenly become.

But it was personal. Gina didn't only want to revive the Finder program, she wanted to learn how to develop those skills herself.

She had had a taste of it. Enough to prove it was real. Enough to make her want to be as proficient at it as she possibly could.

Her brief brush with psychic knowing had saved her life and Mrs. Byers's. It felt like a flaccid muscle inside her mind that she never even knew was there. But now that she did know, she wanted to train it and strengthen it and let it come out of where it had been hiding and take its proper place at the front of her brain.

"People are going to think you're crazy," Hank said.

"Don't really care," Gina answered.

"It's a bunch of old people."

Gina laughed. "That's your argument?"

Hank Alterra closed the file and handed it back to Gina. "I can give you the title, but probably not the raise. Not for something like this. It's like someone asking to be in charge of the kennel for the sniffer dogs. Maybe a lot of fun, but not a lot of glory."

Gina drummed her fingers on top of the file folder. They made a hollow thumping noise. "So I can do it?"

"Restart the division?" Hank shrugged. "Why not. I didn't see her in there, but I used one of them once. Lady named Chancy Wainwright."

"Sorry," Gina said, "she died about five years ago."

Hank nodded. "Weirdest thing. I had this case where I was sure an ex-Marine was selling secrets to the Russians. But I could never catch him at it. Guy always looked squeaky clean. But I just *knew*, you know?"

Gina nodded. She knew.

"I was embarrassed for anyone to find out, but I was desperate after a while. So I trucked down to the third floor and talked to the old head of the division. Guy named Whitling. Still around."

"Ted Whitling," Gina said. "I've met him." She was surprised to see him listed as the former head of the Finders division. Maybe she was a bad judge of age, but she thought he was in his mid-thirties now. That would have made him mid-twenties when the old Agency director shut the program down. Too young. That wasn't how this place worked. You didn't get made head of a division—even a fringe one—unless you'd put in some real years.

"So I told Whitling my problem," Hank went on. "And it was kind of like a dating service. He matched me. Said with her particular skills, Chancy Wainwright was my best bet."

The door to the conference room opened. Hank's assistant stuck his head in. "They want you up on six," he said. "About fifteen minutes ago."

Hank sighed. "Coming." He stood and took his half-full cup back to the coffee station. He dumped it in the trash.

"Long story short," Hank said. His assistant had left again and closed the door behind him. Gina didn't want a shortened story. She wanted the whole thing. But she would take what she could get.

"The guy had a little implant," Hank said. He pointed just above his left hip. "Right here. Some kind of plastic material, so it never showed up on any kind of metal detector. It was…" Hank seemed embarrassed to say it. "Kind of space age. That's the best I can call it. It wasn't anything anyone had seen before. We had it analyzed all over the place."

"But Chancy Wainwright found that for you?" Gina asked.

Hank chuckled. "Don't get offended. Stand up. I'm going demonstrate what she did."

Gina stood in front of him. Hank closed his eyes and mimed lunging straight at her, fast, like a racehorse out of the gate. His hands were like claws as he reached out and grabbed Gina on either side of her hips. Hank opened his eyes and let go again and stepped back to give Gina distance.

"It was like she would have dug it out with her fingernails if I'd let her," Hank said. "She was on *fire.* This nice little old lady, but she was *pissed.* Like she'd seen the whole thing flash through her mind right then. All the treason that guy had been doing. All the damage he'd already done."

"So what happened?" Gina asked.

"Mr. Ex-Marine wasn't too keen on someone going straight in to his implant. Even though Ms. Wainwright only grabbed him outside his clothes, he obviously knew the gig was up. We had him. He pushed her and tried to run away, but I had agents stationed all around. I caught Chancy before she fell to the ground. I could feel her shaking, she was so angry."

"So here's my question," Gina said. "Would you have found that implant anyway, without her? If you'd just worked the case a little longer?"

"Truthfully?" Hank said. "No way, no how. It was a really slick job. Unless the guy went in for surgery and some doctor was poking around, I don't know how any of us were supposed to find it. Ever."

Gina nodded. It was what she wanted to hear.

Both for herself, professionally, restarting an unpopular division, and personally, as someone who wanted exactly those skills and more.

Hank Alterra opened the door. He had already stayed too long.

"It'll mess with your mind," he told Gina. "Just be aware of that."

"Okay. I will. Thanks."

Hank left. Gina reached over and closed the door.

And then she gave in to the big grin that had been wanting to break free ever since she got the okay.

Maybe it was career suicide. Maybe it would mess with her mind. Maybe she would hate giving up field work to manage a group of sensitives, psychics, and freaks.

But she didn't think so. Not when she aspired to be one of those sensitives herself.

It was time to regather the group. Get the whole gang back together.

The Finders Division was alive again.

Gina had work to do.

BELIEVER

1

Meeting at forty-one thousand feet made the most sense.

Alice Kern sat in one of the soft tan leather seats inside Major Zimholt's private jet and waited for her former colleague from the Agency, Gina Firenzi, to hurry aboard.

Even after six consecutive months of doing it this way, Alice was still always tense during the pickups and drop-offs. Four different assassins had already tried to kill her in the space of one week last December—why, Alice still didn't know—and there was always a moment before Gina's tall Amazon-like frame filled the jet doorway when Alice wondered if someone else would appear instead and try to gun her down.

It was why she, the pilot Arnie Camper, and the cabin steward Bruce always came armed on the flight.

Gina would be carrying too, ready in case anyone might be waiting for her when she deplaned a few hours later. She had already taken a knife in her back last December from one of the assassins trying to get past her on his way to Alice. And someone else had tried to kill Gina just a few weeks after that while she pursued one of Alice's leads.

As careful as the two of them tried to be, there was always obviously a risk. But the meetings were too important to miss. Alice and Gina had made real progress in their investigations over the past few months. And they could no longer communicate through the Agency network. Alice had learned her lesson. That was how at least one of the assassins had found where she was hiding at what was supposed to be a secure military base.

Using his jet had been Major Zimholt's idea. A place for Alice and Gina to meet face-to-face, without having to go somewhere public where they might be followed.

Alice had been surprised when Gina first reached out to her back in February, in part because Alice assumed the Agency was done with her. She hadn't heard from anyone at her old job since she went underground with Major Zimholt's group. No one was paying her salary anymore. No one was checking in. She wondered if the Factory, Major Zimholt's hidden facility in the Wasatch

Mountain Range above Salt Lake City, Utah, was really so secure that no one even from Agency could find out where she was.

Alice adjusted to her new, isolated workplace. She spent her days doing exactly what she had been doing before as an analyst: delving into research, following leads, trying to understand the larger picture of who was behind the murder of her parents by creating a mosaic of smaller, sometimes random-appearing pieces. Without access to the Agency's extensive network, she could no longer follow live investigations, but the Factory had its own internal database that was filling in pieces Alice didn't even know she was missing.

Including the secret her parents had been keeping from her all of Alice's life. But there was even more to know than that. Always more. Alice kept following the bread crumbs.

Then one day Arnie Camper gave a quick knock on the door of the second-floor computer room and stuck his head in.

"Message for you," he said in greeting. Camper always had places to go, things to do. He didn't waste his words. He was a test pilot both for the military, at a secret base called the Aviary, and at the Factory, flying Major Zimholt's experimental crafts. He also occasionally piloted Major Zimholt's private jet.

"Gina Firenzi wants a meet," Camper said. "This week. Up for it?"

"Y-yeah," Alice said in surprise. But it was a good surprise. She didn't know Gina well, but she liked her. She liked the senior investigator's confidence. And even though Alice had been the one to kill the assassin who attacked Gina and then her, Gina seemed competent and safe. Alice had the feeling Gina Firenzi was someone reliable to have around in a crisis.

"Any day," Alice told Camper. "Thursday?"

"Thursday," he confirmed. "Nine." Then he shut the door on the computer room and was gone.

Thursday morning Alice was ready early, not really knowing what to expect. She had coffee and a banana and was showered and dressed by eight. She could see from the camera feed showing the weather outside the Factory that the sunlight was still barely creeping over the top of the mountains. The temperature was below zero. She waited in her room until she couldn't stand just sitting around any longer. Freezing or not, she would rather head outside and wait for the sunshine. She bundled up and went.

She had left her old apartment back in San Diego in a hurry, after shooting the first of the series of assassins, the one who broke in during the middle of the night. Although later someone from the Agency had packed a garbage bag filled with some of her clothes, Alice's choice of outfits was still fairly limited. Gone were the clothes she used to wear into the Agency office, the navy slacks and Oxford button-downs and the navy jacket and black dress shoes.

Now the best Alice could do to dress for her meeting was put on her black jeans, a long-sleeved yellow T-shirt, her black fleece vest, and a pair of black waterproof rubber-soled boots from the supply room at the Factory.

She hadn't brought any clothing for the snow. She didn't have any. And when she left San Diego she had no idea she'd end up in the winter mountains. But the supply room at the Factory was like a small department store. Both Alice and her friend Marnie Stemple outfitted themselves with the kind of gear and clothing they needed, including long down coats for when they wanted to leave the unground facility and go up top, outside.

Properly weather-proofed, Alice climbed the metal steps from the Factory, pushed open the heavy door, and stepped outside into the frigid February air.

And now, once a month, never on the same date or the same day of the week, Alice made that same trek up top to find Camper waiting for her, warming up the Major's jet. It was a faster process now in the summer. Alice still wore jeans and T-shirts to their meetings, but a pair of light hikers now took the place of snow boots.

Major Zimholt's jet was a kind of luxury Alice still wasn't used to. She was twenty-six and had lived modestly her whole life. Back in San Diego, she used to live in a studio apartment and drove an eleven-year-old Honda. She bought her clothes at discount stores. Not because she couldn't afford better, but because she didn't want expensive things. That just wasn't how she was raised.

Her family of three had always lived comfortably. Alice's mother was an emergency room doctor and her father was a systems engineer. But her parents never seemed interested in having the latest of anything, in showing off in any way, in competing with what anyone around them had. Alice was the same way. She liked to live simply. Since coming to the Factory to hide, she certainly got her wish.

Now she lived in a single room on the second underground floor, with just enough space for a bed and a few other pieces of furniture, and with a bathroom smaller than the one in her old studio apartment. No kitchen. She shared a communal kitchen if she wanted to cook for herself, and otherwise ate from the cafeteria on her floor.

Marnie was still her only real friend there, although Marnie seemed to have made friends of her own over the past few months. But Alice wasn't much for socializing, even though there were hundreds of other people to choose from who lived and worked at the Factory, along with occasional outsiders who cycled in and out. So far Alice was still discovering who people were and what they did one by one as she had any reason for inter-acting with them.

She used to be social. She used to be friendly and outgoing. She used to be a lot of things. But a gunman had changed everything six years ago, when Alice was twenty years old and a junior in college. She watched the news of a mass shooting and somehow *knew* her parents were in that crowd. The police showed up later to confirm it.

They claimed it was just a random shooting, but Alice had a feeling about that too. She never believed their theory, even though she didn't have a good reason why. But lately, as she found out more about her parents from the files in the database at the Factory, Alice felt more certain than ever that she was right.

Her parents weren't just random people. Someone wanted Dr. Aurora Kern and Will Kern dead. Alice was going to prove it. And then hunt down the people responsible and make sure they paid, one way or another.

The jet was beginning its descent. Alice leaned back into the soft leather armchair and corralled her impatience.

She was sitting alone in the back half of the jet, the part set up like an expensive office suite with eight leather armchairs that swiveled and reclined, and glossy wooden tables set up between the pairs.

The front half of the cabin was a lounge area with

two soft leather couches that could fold out into beds. Alice was never on the jet long enough to need that, but she could imagine how much nicer that would be than some of the red-eyes she had flown in coach.

There were always fresh flowers in a vase near the front of the cabin. Today it was filled with white daisies. Alice's favorites. And there was always a meal, usually some kind of delicious lunch, served on actual china plates with real silverware.

Even if Alice still couldn't get used to all the luxury, she knew that Gina loved it. Especially the in-flight lunches. A little dose of gourmet dining to break up the stale coffee and sandwiches-on-the-run that normally fueled her day.

The jet rolled to a stop. Bruce opened the door and unfolded the short set of steps. Gina jogged up them and entered the cabin. She gave Bruce a friendly touch on the shoulder and called out a greeting to Camper, the pilot. Then she strode back to the rear of the cabin as Bruce retrieved the steps, closed the door, and Camper began taxiing to lift off again.

Gina sank into the seat across from Alice and pulled the cross-body strap of her khaki document bag up over her head. She set the bag on the seat beside her. Gina was at least ten years older than Alice, in her mid- to late-thirties, with shoulder-length curly brown hair she kept tugged back into a low ponytail. She wore dark athletic pants and a pale blue zip-up shirt that made it look like she had just come in from a run. Maybe she had. Gina seemed the type to work out several times a day. She was tall and fit and muscular in a way that made Alice feel puny whenever she stood beside her.

But it also gave Gina an aura of strength that made Alice feel like she could relax in the investigator's presence. As if Alice could let down her guard for at least a short time, knowing that Gina would have her back.

"We might need to start meeting every two weeks," Gina said. "A month is too long to wait."

Alice was glad to hear it. She felt cut off from people like her. She missed the energy of working around other analysts and investigators at the Agency. She loved these sessions with Gina when the two of them could brainstorm and strategize. Twice a month would be great.

Gina dug into her document bag and pulled out a stack of files that made Alice's pupils dilate. So much information. There would be photos and documents and copies of case files in there—Alice couldn't wait to dive in.

She had a stack of documents too, although not nearly that large. She brought them in an orange day pack she got from the supply room at the Factory. The pack came filled with gear for a short mountain expedition: two-liter water bladder, first aid kit, rain poncho, titanium box for food. Alice left them all in her room and filled the space with paperwork instead.

"You first," Alice said.

"Okay. Let's start with him." Gina pulled a photo-graph out of the file folder on top of the stack and slid it across the polished table.

Alice caught her breath. Of course she knew the man in the photo. Gina would too. He was the man who had attacked them with a knife in a bookstore back in December. The one who had stabbed Gina in the back, puncturing her lung, and then tried to kill Alice.

But Alice killed him instead.

"We knew his name from his fingerprints," Gina said. "But guess what else we know now?"

She opened the top file folder again and removed four more color photographs. Mug shots. Alice studied each of the faces.

"Know any of them?" Gina asked.

"None. I've never seen them in surveillance photos or in person." Alice looked across the table at Gina. "So who are they?"

"Part of the same brotherhood," Gina said. "A small cell operating out of LA. All of them suspected of multiple hits."

Alice returned to the first photograph of a black-haired brute named Utkin. He had worn glasses in the bookstore. Maybe because he thought they made him look studious so he could blend in better.

"Lavrev?" Alice asked. It was a name she had first heard from Major Zimholt. According to the Major, Lavrev was a Russian oligarch who was head of the largest Russian syndicate. Major Zimholt thought it was Lavrev who hired the first assassin, a man named Danic, to come after Alice. But so far neither Alice nor Gina had found firm proof of that.

Gina was also looking into connections between Lavrev and the second assassin, Utkin. She hadn't found anything concrete as of their last meeting, but Alice assumed she must have more now. If Gina had four new photographs to lay out, it must mean she had a story to tell.

And she did.

Just not one that Alice expected or wanted.

2

Lunch was served. For the moment, nothing else mattered. At least not to Gina. She was starving.

And she was grateful for the interruption. She still wasn't sure how to introduce the topic at hand. She had rehearsed several openings: *I meant to tell you, I'm head of a new division now ... Okay, I need you to keep an open mind....*

But so far nothing felt right. She hoped she would know her opening when she found it.

Bruce the cabin steward looked distinctly like an Army Ranger to Gina. She liked the type. Not so brawny they could barely fold their arms, but solid like a chunk of marble and quick on their feet.

He set out the fancy plates and cloth napkins and

water glasses for two. No wine glasses. Gina wasn't much of a drinker, and when she did indulge, beer was her liquid of choice.

She was more of a coffee junkie, and the coffee Bruce served was always excellent. Also in fancy cups, although Gina would have preferred a good tall mug.

Lunch was a Caprese salad with cold slices of mozzarella and fresh tomatoes and basil, splashed with what she could have sworn was homemade Italian dressing.

Bruce followed it with warmed eggplant sandwiches on slices of French bread with more mozzarella melted and oozing from the center.

Gina knew that Bruce didn't cook the fine meals himself—at least she assumed he didn't—but damn if she didn't feel like taking him home after these flights and installing him in her cozy little condo.

"Thanks," she told him when he finally took away their plates and returned with a full carafe of fresh coffee. Alice seemed faintly amused by the longing look Gina gave him as he walked away.

"Anyway," Alice said.

"Anyway," Gina agreed. She brushed away the crumbs from her sandwich and grabbed the top folder off the pile she had moved onto the seat beside her. She opened it again and spread the four new photos out for Alice to see.

"So what magic did you use?" Alice asked.

Gina knew her opening when she saw it.

"Funny you should say that," she said. "Let me show you something."

She pulled out a plain brown mailing envelope large enough to contain the photos. She handed it to Alice.

"Hold it up to the light," Gina said. "Can you see into it?"

Alice held up the envelope, checked it, shook her head.

Gina took the envelope back and slid the photo of Utkin, the assassin from the bookstore, into it.

"Okay, check again," Gina said.

Alice repeated the exercise. Again she shook her head. "Can't see anything."

Gina cleared her throat. She knew she should have told Alice her news months ago, but she just hadn't found the right way to do it.

But now she was committed. She could already imagine Alice's reaction. Gina had been seeing it on her fellow investigators' faces ever since her new assignment was announced back in February.

Better to start with the lights and razzle dazzle before giving Alice the punch line.

"So imagine this," Gina said. "I give this envelope to someone with this same picture inside and I ask them where this person was on a specific date and a specific time."

Alice raised her eyebrows. Gina knew she must guess where this was going.

"And this person tells me—actually, doesn't tell me, but tells one of my investigators—that inside the envelope is a picture of a man whose name is Oleg Utkin, he lives at such and such address, he's thirty-seven, all sorts of details, and at that date and time he was in a certain bookstore at this address, et cetera."

Alice gave her a skeptical look. "Okay, so … what's the trick? Plus we already know all that."

"And then this person tells us," Gina continued, "that Oleg Utkin is there at the bookstore to kill someone named Alice Kern—"

Alice sat up straight. "No."

"Yes," Gina said, smiling. The intensity on Alice's face was just what she hoped to see. "And furthermore, he was there at the direction of someone named Simon—"

"Simon?" Alice said. "Who's Simon? We don't know any Simon yet."

Gina held up her finger. "Wait. And then my person also tells us the names of four other men—" Gina gestured to the remaining four photos. "—and gives us their names too. And they check out. Criminal records, known associates, current whereabouts. All of it. These are our guys."

"Wow," Alice whispered. She gaped at Gina with her dark brown eyes. "I can't believe it." Then she smiled and held up her hand. "Well done!"

Gina slapped the offered hand. "Not the whole pie, but certainly a nice juicy slice."

"So who is this person?" Alice asked. "Some informant?"

"Mm, not exactly." Gina stalled by gathering the photos back into a nice neat stack. She slid them and the plain brown envelope back into their proper folder.

"Gina…" Alice was looking at her with a critical eye. "What's going on?"

"Ever heard of the Finders Division?" Gina asked.

"No. Should I?"

"I'm head of it now. It was disbanded several years ago, but I've reactivated it. Gathered all the Finders again—at least the ones who are still alive."

"What are Finders?" Alice asked.

"They … see things. Sometimes at a distance. Sometimes even in the past. Like my friend Mrs. Byers." Gina patted the top of the folder. "She's the one who found these scum for us."

Alice slumped back into her seat. "What are you telling me? These are psychics?"

"Some of them," Gina said. "Some do what's called Far Seeing. It's actually pretty scientific—"

"Gina—"

Gina held up her hand. The one that had so recently slapped against Alice's in celebration. "I know. I've heard it, believe me. But let me remind you of something."

Gina had come prepared. She was glad she'd thought of it. Because she had been the one to introduce Alice to the idea of another anomaly about seven months ago. Gina had to do it from her hospital bed while recovering from Utkin's knife wound to her lung.

She had given Alice a set of her own personal comic books featuring one of Gina's favorite heroines, the mighty female warrior Lenna. In the final installment of the series, Lenna returned from the dead as an avenging angel, complete with wings.

Gina didn't say it at the time, but she already knew that Alice was about to meet a real-life woman who was able to fly. Marnie Stemple. No wings on that one, but from what Gina had heard, Marnie could take off from a running start, flap her arms, and actually get herself airborne.

It was Marnie Stemple's photograph that Gina now pulled out of a separate file.

She slid it across the table to Alice.

Alice looked at it. "So?"

"So, if I had told you that night in the hospital, *Hey, Alice, you're about to meet a flier, get ready!* you would have looked at me the same way you are now. But you came around, didn't you? Because you saw her with your own eyes."

Alice took a sip of coffee. She didn't answer right away.

Gina topped off her own cup from the carafe and sat back to enjoy it while she watched Alice wrestle with the new facts.

"So you're telling me this person—Mrs…"

"Byers," Gina said.

"Byers took that envelope from you—"

"Or one like it," Gina said. "And not actually from me. I didn't want to influence any of her answers. I had one of my investigators do the interview. I watched from another room."

It was part of Gina's double-blind protocol. She had read about it in the old files she researched about the previous incarnation of the Finders Division. One person would select the targets—they might be photographs, a name on a slip of paper, coordinates to a location along with a specific time and date when something significant took place there—and then a separate interviewer who knew nothing about what was inside the envelope would ask the Finder, like Mrs. Byers, the questions.

What do you see?

What is the person's name?

What do you see that person doing?

Who else is there?

Why is this person doing what you are seeing?

A skilled interviewer could act spontaneously and go with the flow of the information. There was no set list of questions. It was a conversation with the Finder to extract as much information as possible before the trail inevitably went cold. Sometimes the Finder might talk for an hour and have a wealth of details to share, but sometimes the interviews ended quickly. The Finder just couldn't seem to latch on to anything significant.

Gina had worked with Mrs. Byers, an elegant older lady in her seventies, several times now, both in the office and out in the field. Mrs. Byers had been with her during a frightening encounter on New Year's Day that led to Gina wanting to revive the Finders Division and learn more about their extraordinary abilities.

Gina wouldn't mind enhancing those abilities in herself. But she wasn't telling anyone that. She doubted she ever would.

But she wasn't just blindly accepting everything the Finders told her. No matter how accurate some of them were. Even Mrs. Byers wasn't a hundred percent on every fact. But she had given Gina so much information now that never could have come out another way, Gina had come to rely on her more and more.

And to keep giving her brown paper envelopes containing clues to some of the Agency's long list of unsolved or stalled cases.

In the past six months, Gina had been able to resurrect at least a dozen cases that had been sitting untouched in metal file cabinets for years.

Her fellow investigators might think the Finders

Division was full of oddballs, but the oddballs were getting it done.

Alice set down her coffee cup. She still slouched back in her seat. Gina recognized the body language. Alice was resistant. Gina needed to fix that before she went any further.

"There's science behind it," she said. "Real science. Out of the former USSR, believe it or not. They took it seriously there back in the sixties, and finally the US started catching up." She leaned forward, closing the distance toward the reluctant Alice. "I know it sounds fringe. But Marnie is real. There are other strange things in this world that are true. Just … hear me out."

Was it too soon? Or was this the right time? Gina had to go with her gut.

She thumbed through the pile of file folders beside her and pulled out another plain brown envelope.

Alice wasn't going to like it. But like it or not, she would have to take it.

"Last week I had my interviewer give this one to Mrs. Byers. Open it."

Alice tore open the sealed flap of the mailing envelope and peered inside. She pulled out the single sheet of paper containing a series of typewritten numbers.

"The top set are coordinates," Gina said. "That's how we identify locations. We don't name them. And the bottom numbers…"

But Alice was already staring at them. Gina didn't have to tell her.

It was the date of Alice's parents' murder. The coordinates were of the location where it happened.

Alice raised her gaze to Gina. She looked hurt, or confused, or maybe even defeated. None of those were the reactions Gina wanted.

Alice asked quietly, "Why?"

Gina needed to turn this around. Get it back on track. Get Alice to see that what Gina did was good.

"Because the Finders know things," Gina said. "They just do. And if I didn't use them, I'd be doing this investigation with one arm tied behind my back."

Alice dropped the paper on top of the envelope and pushed both of them back toward Gina. She got up from her seat. "I need a break. I have to think about this."

Gina didn't try to stop her. Maybe a break was a good idea. Let Alice take time to see that what Gina was offering her was progress. Real progress after Alice had been working on her parents' case mostly by herself for over the past year. Gina wanted to make a real contribution. And she had. Or at least, Mrs. Byers had.

Alice made her way toward the back of the plane to the bathroom. She opened the wooden door and disappeared inside. The lock snicked into place.

Gina let out a sigh. She wasn't sure if that was how she expected it to go, or whether it had gone well or not.

She didn't know anything. She was just trying. That

was all she could do lately. Just throw out her line on the ocean and see what big fish she might be able to catch.

Finding the person or people behind the Kerns' murder would be an awfully huge fish. Maybe not in the scheme of things at the Agency level, but for Alice Kern. Gina wanted to help her.

As long as Alice would let her do it.

3

The jet's bathroom was nicer than the one Alice used to have in her apartment. Not much smaller, either. There was a walk-shower, a slatted wooden bench with plush white towels left rolled up and waiting, a porcelain sink embedded in what might be a granite counter top, and another vase of fresh flowers, this time white roses.

Alice leaned over the sink and stared at her face in the large round mirror.

Her mother's face. Aurora Kern was Filipino. Alice had her same dark brown skin, dark eyes, and long brown hair. She knew there were shapes to her features that came from her father's Germanic side. But any time Alice wanted to remember what her mother looked like, she only had to glance into a mirror.

It was tempting. So tempting. To believe in the fairy tale Gina was offering.

Alice used to believe—or at least enjoy—all sorts of fantasy and science fiction stories. She and her mother loved indulging in movie nights when they'd fill up on all sorts of heroic fantasies—movies with wizards and elves and immortals, martial arts flicks where warriors could soar through the air, land on their feet, vanquish every evil foe.

But reality came crashing down. Alice could hardly bear to remember how naïve and impressionable she used to be. It wasn't a sweet memory, it was a flaw. Maybe if she had been more worldly, tougher, she could have handled her parents' deaths without completely falling apart.

Other people lost loved ones. Alice wasn't unique. But her heart had suffered such irrevocable damage, she knew she would have to be careful all the rest of her life to hold the pieces together by their flimsy tattered remains. She was like a tightrope walker conscious of the brute force of every gust of wind.

She wanted to know. She didn't want to know. She wanted to know if it was real.

But if this Mrs. Byers was just a fortune teller, some charlatan—or not even charlatan, but just some misguided fantasist who believed in her own hype—then Alice couldn't afford to listen to a word of it. She couldn't afford to let herself believe what wasn't true.

Because if Gina was about to tell her a name. Or give her some details of the killing that Alice hadn't found out on her own. Then that information would be inside Alice's head forever from then on. And she might be so misled she would never find the real trail again. She would never really solve her parents' murder.

But of course she wanted to know. Dear God. If it were only that simple.

Alice had never told anyone—she could hardly stand to know it herself—but in the months after her parents' death, she began a private, secret search among the various mediums in the San Diego area. People who claimed they could communicate with the dead. That they could channel them and let the deceased actually speak through them to their loved ones left behind.

Alice looked at their websites. Read their testimonials. Researched complaints against them. Looked for any sign that even one of them could be trusted. That the purported medium wasn't just taking advantage of people in grief.

And finally Alice chose one. Not very scientifically. She liked the woman's picture. The soft look in her eyes. Her sympathetic face. She looked kind and motherly. Alice found herself staring at the woman's picture day after day, and then finally she found the courage to schedule an appointment.

The experience was surreal.

The woman looked exactly like her picture. No

makeup, slightly homely, but with a kindness that came through her gaze.

The woman, Claudine, reached out both her hands to take Alice's between them. Her touch was warm and comforting. Alice was afraid she might start crying just because of that. She had been resisting all the people around her who constantly offered their condolences and asked if she was all right. Of course she wasn't all right. But she always put up a brave front and got rid of the well-wisher as soon as possible. She stood back when they came in for a hug. She didn't want to be held. What she wanted was for none of it to have ever happened.

But Claudine was a stranger, and somehow her warmth felt right to accept. Alice let Claudine lead her into the small and tidy house, into a small dining room with an old-fashioned polished table. There were already two water glasses sitting on coasters in front of two facing chairs. Alice sat on the near one and Claudine went around the table to sit across from her.

Alice's heart was racing. Was she doing the right thing? What would her parents think of this? Would they try to make her stop, would they tell her she was being foolish?

She could imagine coming here with her mother. Maybe as a Mother's Day gift or a birthday present. A fun mother-daughter outing, just something different, a lark, just to see what a medium actually did.

Instead Alice sat alone, heart leaping, her breath feeling hard and ragged in her throat.

"Just relax, dear," Claudine told her. She was in her sixties, maybe, short and a little overweight, with frizzy gray hair held back from her face with a black stretchy hairband.

"I've never done this before," Alice said.

"It's all right," Claudine said. "Nothing to be afraid of."

Claudine reached across the table, inviting Alice to do the same. The surface was wide enough that their fingers barely met.

Alice wondered why Claudine did the session in here, rather than somewhere where she could sit closer to her client. But Alice continued lengthening her arms across the table, anxious now to find even the slightest grip so Claudine wouldn't let go.

"Thank you," Claudine said. "That's all." She retracted her arms and folded her hands together in front of her on top of the table. Alice reluctantly retracted her arms too and placed her hands on her lap.

The form Alice filled out to schedule the appointment asked only for her first name. No last name, no details about who she wanted to contact. Alice appreciated that. It meant Claudine couldn't look her up ahead of time.

Payment was in cash at the appointment, so Claudine didn't have Alice's credit card information either. It seemed like a clean system.

Alice could have used a fake name, and she almost did, but she decided if she was going to do this, she should do it all the way. Not lie, but also not offer any information during her session. Just let Claudine "read her" and see if she could channel the deceased persons Alice was seeking.

"Let me look at you, dear," Claudine said. Her gaze was still soft, just like in her picture on her website, but now it felt penetrating as she stared into Alice's eyes.

Alice wanted to look away. She might not have minded it when she was younger, but after everything that had happened, she realized she felt very sensitive about being seen.

But if she was going to do this, she should do it. Alice kept her gaze steady on Claudine's for what felt like five minutes straight.

Then finally Claudine whispered, "Thank you," and she closed her eyes and began breathing deeply.

Alice sat through several long, tense minutes, again wondering whether she should have ever come here. The price was reasonable—just two hundred dollars, where some other mediums charged five hundred or more—and Claudine seemed normal and down to earth, but this was still so far out of Alice's comfort range it was hard to stay in the high-backed wooden chair and not bolt for the front door.

Then Claudine's voice came softly again, saying, "They passed not long ago." She wrinkled her brow. "Oh, I'm so sorry. How tragic. You must have been devastated."

Alice pressed her lips together. She would not speak. If this was a trick, it was the easiest one to see. Claudine would say something general—*How tragic. How sad*—and the grieving person would spill their guts and maybe even share some of the details of what made the death so awful.

"Your mother is here," Claudine said. The medium raised her hand into the air and stroked it downward a few times, as if Aurora Kern herself might be trying to stroke Alice's hair. It was a gesture Alice recognized.

Alice caught the sound that wanted to erupt from her throat. She swallowed it down hard before it could turn into a sob. She clenched her hands together on her lap. She sat upright and as still as possible. If this was a trick, she wasn't falling for it.

"And your father," Claudine said.

Maybe she did research Alice after all. Maybe she had some way of locking into the location of Alice's computer when she made the appointment. Then it would be easy to find the newspaper articles about the shooting. They went on and on for months.

"He's showing me … he's showing me…" Claudine wrinkled her brow again. "It's an egg timer. Does that mean anything to you?"

Alice covered her mouth with her hand. Claudine's eyes were still closed. Alice tried to keep it together.

But yes, she recognized an egg timer. It was part of a game she played with her father. Name as many of X as you can in two minutes. Capital cities, names of rivers, songs that begin with *S*, foods that begin with *M*—it could be anything. Just for the fun and speed of it. To see who could win by naming more.

Sometimes they wrote their answers down, sometimes they shouted them out at each other, keeping track by counting on their fingers. Either of them could call for the game at any time—during commercials, just before guests were about to arrive for a party, first thing in the morning before her father had had his coffee—the more inconvenient, the better. Because the rule was you couldn't refuse. Will Kern used that to his advantage when Alice was anxious to leave the house to go out with her friends. Her father would pull out the egg timer, and Alice would have to stop and play. She pretended to be annoyed, but the truth was she loved it. It was their tradition, carried over from her childhood, all the way up until Will Kern died. Alice could remember playing it with him when she stopped by the house to visit her parents just a few weeks before the shooting.

Name dogs from movies. Go.

Lassie, Air Bud, Hundred and One Dalmations—

That's the name of the movie, not the dog!

—Benji, Marley, White Fang—

"Alice?" Claudine said quietly. "Does an egg timer mean anything to you?"

Alice couldn't resist. "Y-yes."

Claudine smiled. "Good. And your mother is here. She says she loves you..."

And now Alice was crying, and from then on it only got worse.

When the session was over, Alice paid Claudine her two hundred dollars and added a twenty dollar tip.

She left Claudine's house with red, swollen eyes and an ache in her chest that felt even more painful than when she arrived.

It was easy to start picking apart everything Claudine said, and everything Alice confirmed. Easy to see how Alice might have been led from one answer to another, feeling her out, reading her, telling her what she wanted to hear.

Except for the egg timer.

That. No one could have found that in an article about the killing, or in any internet search about Alice Kern. The information had to have come from another source.

Alice mulled over the session detail by detail for days and weeks afterward.

Was it true? Was any of it true?

And even if it was, what had she really learned?

Claudine, speaking on behalf of Will and Aurora

Kern, assured Alice over and over how much they loved her.

Yes, it hurt like a stab wound to her heart to hear it said. Alice sobbed. All her plans about being stoic and unreadable fell apart so quickly, she wondered why she thought she would be able to do it at all.

She was a wreck. The session felt as if all it did was open Alice's barely-closed wounds. She shut herself away. Didn't answer her phone, texts, emails, ignored knocking and sometimes pounding on her door.

When the commotion became too much, she drove to the beach and walked for hours.

So no, it hadn't helped her at all. In some ways it had made her grief far worse than before. Because now all she wanted to do was go back to Claudine's house and pay her two hundred dollars a day just to hear words that any medium could fake if she wanted to.

We miss you. We love you. We're so proud of you.

And now Gina. Offering something that might be equally alluring and maybe equally untrue.

But Marnie Stemple is real.

Just like the egg timer was real.

Alice gripped the edges of the sink and leaned forward and rested the top of her head against the cold mirror. When she pulled away there was a smudge where she would normally look for her mother's eyes staring out through hers.

Alice sank onto the slatted wooden bench across

from the shower. She leaned back against the wall and caught her breath. She knew what she had to do, she just needed another few minutes. Two minutes, to be exact.

Set the egg timer. Two minutes to name all the reasons why you don't want to do this. Go.

Because it might be fake. It might be real. I might learn more than I'm ready to know. I might have to hear about their last minutes. I don't want to know. Were they afraid? Were they in pain? Would Gina's Finder be able to tell me? Could I stop her from telling me? She's not even here. It's already done.

What would my father do now? What would my mother do, if I was the one who had been shot? Would they want the details? Or would they rather let me go in peace?

There is no peace. There won't be. Not until I know the reason they were killed.

Dammit, don't be a coward. Go out there and fight.

Alice stood from the bench and went back to the sink. She turned on the faucet and splashed cold water against her face. She patted it dry with the soft white towel. She leaned over and smelled the white roses in the vase. Stalling, but only because she had already made up her mind. She could afford to take a moment to smell the roses.

She unlocked the door and made her way back along the carpeted floor to her fancy seat. Gina was enjoying a slice of some kind of chocolate cake on a clear glass plate.

Alice sat across from her and held out her hand for

the envelope again. Gina patted her mouth with her cloth napkin and held up her finger for Alice to wait.

"I have the transcript," Gina said. "Of the whole interview. You can read it, or I'll summarize."

"Tell me again," Alice said. "Why should I think this is real?"

"Because I'm the only one who knew what was on that paper inside the envelope," Gina said. "The interviewer and Mrs. Byers went in blind. No one read her the coordinates or the date. She didn't touch the envelope. No one opened it. The interviewer placed it on the table in front of her, and Mrs. Byers just looked at it."

"And then…"

Gina finished a sip of coffee. "And then she started telling the interviewer what she saw at that place on that date. I'll be honest, parts of it are very rough. You might not need to know everything. Like I said, I have the transcript if you want it—"

"Summarize," Alice said.

She hated to feel cowardly, but she had already had her heart beaten to a bloody pulp. She trusted Gina to extract the pertinent information for the case, while sparing Alice the worst of her pain.

"Bottom line, you were right," Gina said. "The targets were Will and Aurora Kern."

Alice sucked in a breath. She wanted to know it and she didn't. But really, hadn't she known it all along? Not with any proof, just a feeling. She couldn't even say why she knew it back when she was twenty. She was still just a child. She didn't know any of the things she knew now after working for the Agency for the past year. But Alice couldn't pretend to be surprised. So she nodded and waited for more.

"We already know the shooter's name. But Mrs. Byers gave us that again. She knew a lot about his preparations for the day. I can extract that from the transcript it you want—"

"No," Alice said. "Just go on. Who hired him? Did Mrs. Byers know?"

"A first name," Gina said. "Apparently that's all the shooter knew."

Alice had a feeling. She blurted out the name.

"Simon."

Gina nodded. "Whoever that bastard is. I'm sorry, but Mrs. Byers couldn't tell us any more about him. I think it's because he was careful the shooter didn't know any more either."

Alice felt weary. And heavy with a fresh new burden. As if she finally opened a door and found a boulder now barring her way. She couldn't lift it, she couldn't go around it or through it. She could only stare at it and wonder what on earth she was supposed to do next.

"So how does this work?" Alice asked. "Is it a dead end? Or is there some other way now to find out who Simon is?"

"We'll find out," Gina promised. "Remember those

four new pictures I showed you. They work for Simon too. We'll keep digging. We'll find him."

Alice brought her hand to her face. She covered her mouth and turned to stare out the window. The sky was light blue and clotted with clouds. She wished now she hadn't eaten any of the lunch. It sat like a brick inside her belly. She wanted to go home.

Home home. Not back to the Factory. Not even back to her little studio apartment in San Diego.

Home to the place that she sold, the place where she grew up. Home to her bedroom, decorated in green and white and overstuffed with books and games and the models she and her father had built together from kits. There was an airplane that took them weeks to figure out. But everything worked and the moving parts moved: propeller, doors, wing flaps, wheels.

It was all packed away. In some storage unit Alice paid for every year. She hadn't been back to look through it since she put the lock on the door and drove away.

She couldn't go back. She could only go forward. That was the truth, as bedrock solid as anything she knew.

Alice turned back to Gina. "Okay. Then we find out who Simon is. Good work, Gina. I mean it."

"I'm sorry," Gina said.

"For what?"

"Maybe I should have asked you first."

Alice shook her head. "I would have said no. And you're right, we'd still be stuck back where we were. At least we've moved forward. I appreciate that."

Gina studied her for a moment. Alice gave her a shrug and her best attempt at a smile.

"None of this is fun," Alice said. "It never will be. You can't be afraid to tell me things I probably don't want to hear."

Gina nodded. "Okay. Got it. But I meant what I said before. I think we should start meeting every two weeks."

"Do they … do they ever talk about me coming back?" Alice asked.

"They do," Gina said. "*I* do. But we still don't think it's safe. Not yet. Give us time. You're a good analyst. We could use you back."

Alice hadn't really expected anything different. Nothing had really changed. If she had been a threat to someone back in December, then she still was. It was why she and Gina were having this conversation high among the clouds rather than at the Agency amid the bustle of investigations.

Alice felt a slight tilt in the pit of her stomach. Camper must be starting another descent. They couldn't hide up here forever. Gina had work to do. So did Alice.

They traded their stacks of files and both stowed them away, Gina in her khaki document bag and Alice in her orange day pack.

"If it was me," Gina said, "I wouldn't read transcript. But I gave it to you anyway. It's your decision."

Alice nodded. She didn't answer. She wasn't sure what she was going to do or what she would say.

When the jet came to a stop on the private runway, Gina pulled out her service weapon and waited at the door with Bruce. But no one was waiting to attack. Maybe no one ever would. Maybe all of these precautions were unnecessary. But four assassins had tried to kill Alice, one of them had stabbed Gina, and someone else had tried to shoot her not long after. It was the nature of precautions to feel unnecessary—until they were. For now, none of them were interested in letting down their guard.

As soon as Gina was safely off, Camper wheeled the jet around and took off again.

Alice had noticed before that it never needed refueling. She knew nothing about jets. Maybe they could fly a whole day on one tank of gas. She had enough things to try to know without adding that one.

As she stared out the window at the slow, puffy clouds, Alice could feel the tightness in her chest gradually ease.

She laid her hand on top of the orange daypack. There were enough documents in there to keep her occupied reading for days. And once she started cross-referencing some of the names with the files in the

Factory database, she might have whole new vistas to explore by the end of the week.

And then maybe Gina would take some of that information and hide it in a plain brown envelope. And maybe Mrs. Byers or one of the other Finders would tell them details they could never expect.

If this was the way it was going to be from now on, maybe Alice should just accept it and not fight it in the least.

There were moments even now when she regretted not going back to see Claudine. Not asking for more, give me more, tell me more.

Maybe her mother would reach out with some private memory of her own. Something that only she and Alice had shared.

Maybe Alice's father would move beyond mentioning just the egg timer, and would tell Alice some truth that she needed to know.

Maybe maybe maybe.

Alice had had enough of maybes. She needed action and facts and truth. She needed to know she was doing what she could, every day, to find out why her parents were gone.

It didn't take a medium to tell Alice her parents loved her and missed her. Alice knew it. Just as they would have known it if she were the one who died.

But if Claudine or Mrs. Byers or someone else could tell Alice what was hiding behind that huge boulder in her way, then she wanted to hear it. She wanted to know it. She was ready.

Simon. Who are you, Simon? I'm going to find you, Simon. I'm going to get you.

Back when Alice was young, maybe nine or ten, she had a lesson one night at the dojo that she never forgot.

It was with her Uncle Edilmark, who was ten years older than Alice's mother and had been born in the Philippines before the family emigrated to America. The other brother, Alice's Uncle Condring, was two years older than that. They were both in their late forties then, about the age Alice's mother was when she was killed, and they were strong and serious and funny at times, and much alike and yet distinctly different.

Uncle Edilmark had the slighter build of the two. He looked more like Alice's mother than the other brother. He kept his thick brown hair long, in a ponytail down his back, like the warriors in martial arts films. He was fast and nimble. His hands could move in a blur, like Bruce Lee's. Watching him spar with the black belts was like watching a cheetah go after gazelles.

Uncle Condring was taller than his other two siblings, and also stocky and solid and practically immovable. He was a stockbroker by day, dojo owner and instructor by night, so he kept his graying hair cut short and corporate-looking for his bosses and clients. Alice was always surprised by how natural he looked in both his business suits and in the heavy black cotton pants and jacket that made up the *gi* he wore in the dojo.

Both of her uncles taught young Alice how to fight in the Filipino style they had learned when they were boys. Then Alice's mother taught her her own techniques for taking down bigger opponents like Alice's uncles.

Alice's mother was sneaky and scrappy. Alice always liked her lessons best.

But the lesson from Uncle Edilmark made a different kind of impression on Alice. One she still applied at times like these when she was feeling overwhelmed and frustrated and lost.

She was working with Uncle Edilmark on improving her blocks against punches to her face. She could react swiftly, get her arm into position in time to deflect the blow, but Alice still couldn't help flinching away. Jerking her head back. She didn't trust her block enough to calmly stand her ground.

Uncle Edilmark identified the problem. He said, "You only think of being attacked. You are thinking what they want to do to you. But you should think of what *you* are doing to *them*."

He told her to see it only from her own side. "Someone has activated you. Someone has woken you up. Now *you* are doing a thing." He pulled her arm up into position. Her fist was tight, ready for the block. "They shouldn't have done it," her uncle said. "Now they must face you. Believe in your power, Alice. *You* are doing a thing."

He backed away, into position, and threw a punch toward her face again.

Alice glared back at him as she raised her forearm into the block. And this time she leaned in. She went for it. She pushed him back with the force of her block. Even though she was only a small girl defending against the punch from a grown man. *She* was doing a thing.

As Camper continued his descent over the Wasatch Mountains, down toward the Factory's hidden airport, Alice could feel the change inside her body. A tilt. A new angle. And she could feel the change in her mind.

She had been on the defensive for over six years now. Reeling. Reacting. Holding so tightly to keeping herself together.

Wanting to know the truth—and afraid of knowing the truth. Why had the two people who meant everything to her been taken away? *Why?* It was a quest she realized now she was afraid of. It was the punch aiming at her face. She would block it because that was what she was trained to do. But she was afraid of it. She still wanted to jerk her head away.

No, *I'm* doing a thing.

Activated. Awakened. Stepping into it. Pushing back.

Pushing, defending, then fighting with all of her skill and might. Not just cowering away from the blows. She had been doing that for too long. Hiding behind her research. Seeking, but then hiding from knowing too much.

None of it on purpose, none of it even punching through to her awareness. It was only now, staring out the jet window to the masses of yellow and purple wildflowers growing all along the hillsides down below, that Alice was willing to see with fresh eyes the change in the seasons. The new growth. The way that winter gave in to the force of a mountain summer. Even up this high in the Wasatch Mountains, where spring had been short and late and barely noticeable until late June, the flowers did come. The snow did melt. The sun did shine, no matter what.

She could move forward. Change. Arise.

Someone has activated you. Someone has woken you up. Now you are doing a thing. They shouldn't have done it. Now they must face you.

They must face her. The four men in Gina's files. Simon, whoever he was. Everyone who was responsible. Every last one of them.

Alice sat up straight. She could feel the strength flowing back into her limbs.

She wasn't afraid of the truth anymore. She would know it all.

She would get back on the mat and fight.

And one day she was going to make this right.

FLIGHT LESSON

The morning air felt warm against Marnie's face. Deliciously warm. She floated through it like swimming through the perfect temperature of a pool. Cooler than body temperature, so it felt refreshing, but with the golden heat of sunshine making her fingers feel soft and nimble.

And she needed them to be nimble. She was still trying a new technique that Hoala taught her a few days ago, and it didn't come naturally. At least not yet.

The Wasatch Mountain Range outside Salt Lake City, Utah, was chock full of the most beautiful alpine wildflowers Marnie had ever seen. Yellow flowers on the mule's ears, purple lupines, coral-colored paintbrushes. Showy asters and delicate white sego lilies and varieties she had never seen before, or maybe just never noticed. Hoala was teaching her to notice.

Marnie Stemple had lived in Utah before, back when she was a teenager. But that was near the red rocks of the canyon lands, not in high mountain forests like this. She had moved around a lot in the past several years, mostly keeping to the West where the climate and the wide open spaces suited her need to fly multiple times a day, but she had never stayed at such a high altitude through winter before. That was new.

After months of more and more snow, and fierce winds that sometimes threatened to slam Marnie into the hard rock surrounding the deep canyons where she loved to fly, suddenly in the middle of April the hillsides began to melt out, revealing dirt and blue-green sage bushes and all the optimistic buds sprouting on bare aspens.

There were still snowy days, but fewer of them. And then everything started greening up. All at once. Like a sped-up nature film. From white to brown to green in a matter of just a few weeks.

And now, in July, it was full-on summer with its long, long days, so many extra hours for flying, and no responsibilities. It was like summer vacation back when she was a kid. Nothing to do but play and try new things.

It had been a long time since Marnie felt free to relax like this. She was twenty-eight, almost twenty-nine, and had been on her own since she was seventeen. On her own and on the run. But she had no desire to run anymore. She couldn't imagine wanting to be anywhere else.

Hoala. All because of Hoala. Marnie's unexpected teacher and friend.

An alien woman from a planet she still hadn't named for Marnie. There were a lot of things Marnie didn't know about her. But she was satisfied with the pace of what Hoala chose to reveal. Marnie knew what it was like to feel pushed and pressured. Hoala didn't do it to her, and Marnie wouldn't do it to Hoala.

Hoala was flying out in front this morning, her pale green skin and long silver hair visible off in the distance. Marnie wore one of her special skin-tight flight suits, the matte gray one this morning, and even though it had a sleek hood that she could pull up to tuck her hair into and keep it off of her face, Marnie was letting it fly free today, like Hoala did.

She was even letting it grow out, rather than cutting it every few weeks to make sure it never obscured her vision. Before, when she might have to escape at a moment's notice, to leave if anyone suspected what she could do, everything Marnie did in her life was built around her safety. She kept very few possessions, since she might have to leave them behind. She always wore clothes that she could fly in—leggings, light-weight sneakers, body-hugging shirts that gave her arms full movement.

Now all she ever needed to wear was one of the flight suits made for her by Major Zimholt, the grandfatherly man who owned the Factory where Marnie was staying with her friend Alice Kern, and comfortable shoes so she could land on rock or dirt or snow or trees. That was all. Like a bird who only needed her feathers and claws.

Hoala flew naked. Her body was slim and androgynous. She had webbing between her fingers and toes and pale green flesh-covered wings like a bat's underneath her arms. When she flew, she glided through the air with a grace Marnie could only envy, and never quite match.

But Hoala was trying to help her improve her technique.

No one had taught Marnie to fly. The skill—what Marnie thought of as her *condition*—came to her one night in the snowy Alaskan wilderness when she was sixteen. Her mother, an anthropologist, studied ancient civilizations. She discovered a secret ritual that gave Marnie the power of flight.

Ultimately, that ritual ruined both of their lives. But even though that was long ago now, Marnie still lived with the effects every moment of every day.

All these years, she hadn't enjoyed flying so much as simply needing to do it. To satisfy the compulsion.

But Hoala was teaching her to love it. To want it. To get better and better at it.

The air seemed to slide past Hoala's hands because of her webbing. Marnie had never paid much attention to her own hands. They were just there, out in front of her or stretched out to her sides, either gliding or helping her swim through the air doing freestyle or the butterfly stroke, just like when Marnie was a little girl on swim team.

But now Marnie was paying attention. She tried to copy the hand position Hoala had shown her. Fingers spread out and relaxed, flat in the air, not bent or scooped, aiming instead of just flaccid. Marnie's hands cramped if she tried to do it too long. She hadn't learned the skill of relaxing them. They were still stiff and tense.

And her feet. Not just hanging behind her or kicking through the air like she used to when she swam, but deliberately still and slightly pointed to make them more aerodynamic.

Hoala didn't use words like aerodynamic. Maybe that wasn't part of her culture's vocabulary. She called it *flight soft*. Letting the air do more of the work. Finding the right currents and then slipping into them and holding a steady, soft position rather than constantly moving her arms or kicking her feet or just generally *trying*. Hoala never seemed to try. She just jumped from heights, spread her arms, melded with the currents of air.

But Hoala wasn't just teaching Marnie how to improve her flying techniques. That was only a recent lesson. And although it was interesting, and useful, Hoala was teaching Marnie something far more important.

How to create hideaways out of what seemed to be the empty air. How to create something out of nothing. At least that was how it seemed to Marnie's human eyes.

She first saw Hoala's art—that was how Marnie thought of it, as an art, although someone else might view it as magic—the night Hoala saved her from freezing to death in a snowstorm. Marnie woke up inside a structure someplace where it was dry and cozy and warm.

It wasn't until the morning, when sunlight streamed through the transparent walls of the pyramid-shaped structure, that Marnie could see they were somehow *inside* the mountain. Up at the top of a peak. Hoala had somehow found a way to burrow inside solid rock and create a transparent and weather-proof room where she and Marnie could rest and look out the see-through walls to the magnificent mountain scenery all around them.

Marnie couldn't do that yet. She secretly doubted she ever could.

But Hoala was trying to teach her—had been trying for seven months now—how to build platforms on branches of trees and then raise transparent walls to form small pyramids in places where Marnie would like to rest from flying for a while, or sit out a storm, or hide from anyone's attempts to find her.

The structures and whatever was inside them were invisible to anyone searching for them, even if someone were standing close enough to touch them. Marnie had done that experiment herself. Unless Hoala brought her inside one of her special shelters, Marnie had no idea where the structure might be.

"I don't understand how you make these," Marnie said after running her hands down the smooth transparent wall of a hideaway Hoala had erected within the boughs of a massive fir tree. "I don't understand what the material is."

Hoala pinched her thumb and forefinger and rubbed them together. "Air. The space between the air." She touched the webbing between her two fingers. "Like this."

Marnie tried to understand the example, but couldn't. It made no sense. The webbing between Hoala's fingers was solid and visible. What was the space between the air supposed to be?

But whatever it was, it was tangible and solid. Solid enough to stand on and to become a floor and walls. There must be some scientific explanation for it—unless it was, in fact, magic—but Marnie didn't dare ask any of the scientists working at Major Zimholt's hidden facility called the Factory. Asking questions might lead to questions in return. And Marnie knew to keep Hoala's existence secret.

From what Marnie gathered, Hoala had lived in the mountains and forests near the Factory for years. Decades. Maybe since the Factory was first built by Major Zimholt's father back in the 1960s.

Why Hoala was here, why she was here *alone*, Marnie still didn't understand. But over time Hoala had been adding to the few tidbits of knowledge Marnie could gain. With patience, maybe one day Marnie would know the whole story.

She could see Hoala up ahead, banking to her right toward a flower-smothered slope. Maybe she would continue her lessons in shelter-building there. Marnie followed along through the waves of wind until she reached the saddle between two high ridges. Hoala stood barefoot among the tall grass and yellow sunflowers with her eyes closed and her face turned into the breeze. Her long silver hair billowed behind her.

As Marnie alighted by her side, Hoala opened her pale green eyelids to reveal eyes that seemed filled with liquid silver. They were oval rather than round, and twice the width of a human's eyes, with small black pupils in the center. The rest of Hoala's facial features were very human-like: a small, straight nose, small rounded ears, and a wide mouth with pale green lips. But it was her eyes that made her so beautiful.

The saddle where they stood was a flat spot between

two ridges thick with old growth of spruce and fir trees. No one would see them here, even if someone flew nearby in one of the Factory's pods. Marnie could practice her shelter-making in private.

Rather than try to build a platform on the branch of a tree, the way Hoala could, or even harder, build a pyramid-shaped shelter inside a solid mountain peak, Marnie was still taking baby steps, trying to construct just a transparent floor on top of flat areas where she didn't have to depend on her platform to keep her aloft.

The lesson began as they always did, with Hoala demonstrating the skill first.

There in the patch of sunflowers, she slowly swept her hand down toward her webbed feet. Marnie could see the effect of the transparent floor now pressing down against the grass and the flowers.

Then Hoala extended her arms out from her sides and drew them up over her head. The pale green wings that attached from her elbows to her lowest ribs fanned out in their triangular shape. Marnie could see sunlight filtering through the thin flesh of the wings.

As Hoala raised her arms, she disappeared from Marnie's sight. That was the effect of the shelter, the hideaway, as Marnie thought of it. A place to disappear, to hide, to rest. Marnie had been inside many of Hoala's shelters by now. They were always the perfect temperature, always cozy, no matter what weather might be raging outside.

Hoala soon reappeared. She could dissolve her shelter walls with a simple sweep of her hand. With that same gesture she removed the platform at her feet. Marnie watched every movement with rapt concentration. One of these days she would be able to do it. Maybe today was the day.

"Quiet your heart," Hoala told her. "Quiet your mind."

Marnie closed her eyes and tried to breathe deeply. But she was always too excited at this point. Too anxious to try it again. Nervous that she would fail just like all the other times.

Hoala's voice came into Marnie's mind. *What are you thinking?*

Too much, Marnie thought back. It hadn't been difficult to learn this way of communicating. From the very beginning Marnie had been able to hear Hoala speaking inside her mind. Marnie answered her out loud at first, but over time it began to feel natural to communicate in Hoala's silent way. It was the only way they could talk as they flew. Not that Hoala was chatty during their flights, but sometimes she wanted Marnie to follow her someplace new, or to see something Marnie might not have noticed. A bird or a flower or a cloud formation off in the distance. The two of them switched back and forth now, from silent to speaking, depending on whether Marnie was relaxed enough to conduct their conversations entirely inside her mind.

Sometimes she felt too amped up to only think and not speak.

But she was working on quieting her mind. All the time now, whether she was with Hoala or not.

Marnie took a deep breath. She opened her eyes. She tried to soften her gaze, the way Hoala taught her. Not stare at the ground like her eyeballs were lasers, not tense up her body as if what she was about to do was hard. Instead, just casually glance at the ground, as if Marnie only intended to admire the flowers and the butterflies winging amongst them. Then just as casually, try to create a shelter.

Marnie held out her right hand, palm up, fingers lightly together. She kept in mind the image of what she wanted to make. A small, transparent platform just large enough to stand on. She gently swept her hand from her left foot to her right, picturing the platform, hoping, wishing this time it would appear.

It did not.

Marnie blew out an impatient breath.

"Tell me what you see," she said out loud to Hoala. "Describe it to me. You said you're using the space between the air. But what is it, exactly? I just don't understand."

Hoala's voice, when she used it, was a comfort to Marnie's ears. Like hearing someone's pure, perfect tones as they sang a beautiful lullaby. "To you the air seems empty," Hoala said. "But it is not. It is made of energy and vitality. Your scientists say it is filled with molecules and atoms. It is that and much more."

Hoala seemed to have a knowledge of science, or at least of what human scientists thought and did. It was one of the things Marnie was curious about. How did Hoala know anything about that?

"Okay," Marnie said, "but how do I turn all that into a shelter?"

"How do you fly?" Hoala asked.

Marnie sighed. She tried not to show her frustration. But how she flew was entirely different. She flew because her mother spoke special words in a special place at a special time. Marnie had nothing to do with it.

"How do you see me now," Hoala asked, "when before you never could?"

The question took Marnie by surprise. She didn't realize there was ever a time when she couldn't see Hoala. She just assumed the alien had never come close enough before. Not before the night when Marnie met her.

"Are you saying you flew near me before the night of the snowstorm?" Marnie asked.

"Many times," Hoala said. "I was happy to see you when you first arrived. Another flier, like me. I waited for you. Some days you never came outside."

The news came as a shock. Marnie felt a pang in her heart. A loss. It meant she could have known Hoala much sooner. She could have been flying with her all along. Marnie didn't know.

"No," she said. "Some days if the weather was bad I just flew inside the Factory."

"When you came outside, I flew with you," Hoala said. "Every time."

Hoala smiled. But Marnie's heart still felt the blow. A loneliness swept through her. Even though Alice Kern was at the Factory, Marnie's first real friend of her adult life, there was still an emptiness that Marnie didn't realize was there until now. Like finding out she was a twin, but it had been hidden from her all her life. Now she longed for the connection and felt robbed of the time she might have already spent getting to know Hoala months ago.

"Why didn't you…" Marnie paused and cleared her throat. She didn't want to appear emotional. Even though she suspected Hoala could already read it inside Marnie's mind. "Why didn't you speak to me? Or show me you were there?"

"It was not my choice," Hoala said. "I have always been who I am. You had to learn to see me."

Marnie remembered her first sight of Hoala inside the hideaway at the top of the peak. Marnie saw her very clearly then, an alien woman with pale green skin, wearing a long loose pale green garment that covered her from neck to ankles. Marnie saw the webbing between her fingers and toes. She could hear Hoala speaking to her inside her mind. Was it true, could she have seen Hoala before if only her eyes knew what to look for?

"Did you ever try to speak to me?" Marnie asked.

"No," Hoala said. "I kept my distance from your mind. How would you have reacted to hear me speaking inside your thoughts?"

Marnie had to admit it. "It probably would have freaked me out. Or I just wouldn't have believed it."

"You needed to learn to see me first." Hoala still stood amidst the sunflowers and grass. "Watch me again." She gestured down to her feet and built a transparent platform there. Then slowly, more deliberately, it seemed, than normal, she extended her arms and raised them gradually up above her head.

There was a shimmer. Like a heat shimmer rising from asphalt on a broiling summer day. Marnie squinted. She could just barely make out Hoala's form. But she could see at least that much, when before Hoala would completely disappear behind the walls of her shelter.

She saw Hoala wave her hand aside, like shooing a fly. The shelter walls dissolved.

"Again," Hoala said. She repeated the process. Slightly faster this time. "Soften your eyes," Hoala told her. Marnie stopped staring so intently. When the pyramid was complete, she could see Hoala within it, like seeing the outline of someone behind a light-colored shower curtain.

Hoala dismissed the shelter again. She stepped out of the flowers and came to sit on the patch of dirt where Marnie stood. Marnie sat down beside her. She felt mentally tired, as if she had just lifted hundred-pound weights using only her brain.

"It is a skill," Hoala told her. "Seeing, flying, making, they are all skills. You can attain any of them."

Marnie appreciated her teacher's confidence. It filled the gaps in her own.

"I'll keep practicing," Marnie said. It was all she could try to do.

The day was warm. Marnie swiped the back of her hand across her sweaty forehead. Her loose hair was plastered against the back of her neck.

Hoala never sweated. She never seemed to get thirsty. Or at least, Marnie never saw her drink. But Hoala seemed mindful of Marnie's human needs.

As she had done many times before, Hoala waved her hand and somehow summoned or created—Marnie wasn't sure which—the silver pitcher of water shaped like a swan. With another wave Hoala's hand came back holding a silver cup shaped like two eggs melded together and leveled at the top to create a rim.

Marnie had seen both of them the night that Hoala rescued her from the snowstorm and brought her inside the shelter to get warm.

Hoala poured her special liquid from the swan's

beak into the cup. Marnie accepted it gratefully and drank it down. It wasn't water, or at least not only water. It was slightly thicker and sweeter, with a tinge of pine flavor to it. It wasn't something Marnie would ever deliberately buy from a shelf of energy drinks at a store, but whenever Hoala offered it, Marnie was glad to take it. It refreshed her unlike anything else and seemed to bring strength to her body and clarity to her mind.

Marnie chugged the liquid down. She returned the empty cup to Hoala, who waved it and the swan-shaped pitcher away into oblivion.

Marnie shook her head. "It's just magic, isn't it? There's no way I'll ever do that."

"If you believe so," Hoala said, "then you are right."

"It can't be that simple," Marnie said. "Just believe that I can do it."

"You believe you can fly," Hoala said.

"Because I can!" Marnie said. Why didn't Hoala understand? Why did they keep going around and around like this, never leading to any real answers?

Hoala was silent for a time. She sat erect with her perfect posture and looked out over the bees and butter-flies amidst the flowers.

Then she said, "Stand up," and she rose gracefully to her feet.

Marnie stood.

"Hold out your hands," Hoala said, demonstrating

with her own. Palms down, fingers spread, showing off the webbing between them.

Hoala touched the tips of her fingers to Marnie's.

A change began to happen.

Like water sliding off one surface onto another, gently, steadily, naturally—

Hoala's pale green skin began to slide off her body and onto Marnie's. Beginning with her fingers. Marnie watched incredulously as her own fingers took on Hoala's webbing. Then the skin continued growing up Marnie's arms. Smoothly, effortlessly, and without any more of a feeling than a breeze blowing across the hairs of Marnie's arm. Softly and gently.

Marnie's matte gray flight suit, already tight against her skin, took on the pale green of Hoala's body. It followed the contours of the flight suit down to Marnie's ankles. Then, instead of growing into the supple booties that covered her feet, they became her own feet, but webbed and light green.

Marnie tucked her hands under each armpit. Hoala's wings were now attached.

And Hoala … Hoala's skin began to shimmer, the way it did inside the pyramid shelter. Marnie watched while the pale green faded from Hoala's face and body and limbs.

In its place, Hoala seemed covered head to foot with a soft yellow light.

No, not covered—*revealed.*

As if the green skin and webbing and wings were just a flight suit Hoala wore.

And this, this yellow light glowing now in the human-like shape standing in front of Marnie—this was the true Hoala. This was what she was.

The yellow form began to change shape. Its arms and legs shortened. Its head sank downward into its shoulders.

It lost any appearance of a human body. It was a glowing yellow oval now, shorter, maybe four feet tall, with nothing to distinguish head from arms from legs from any of it. Like watching a reverse nature film where the bird became a fledgling again and then finally returned its egg.

What do you see? Hoala asked Marnie inside her mind.

A miracle, Marnie thought back.

Then Marnie felt a grip at her back, low on her spine, as if Hoala had an invisible hold on her there. Marnie felt her body rise off the ground. Then Hoala flung her into the air with so much force Marnie had no choice but to jerk her arms outward to try to catch herself to keep from falling.

The wings caught the wind. Marnie raised and lowered her arms. She straightened her fingers of her webbed hands, just like Hoala had been trying to teach her, and she felt the wind respond as it glided across her wrists and along her arms.

There was too much going on all at once. Marnie's

mind felt like a rat's nest of wires. This one going this way. That one crossing behind. Hold on, hold on, let me take them apart one by one—

The flight suit. This was just a flight suit. A better one, way more advanced than the already futuristic one Major Zimholt had designed.

It fit Marnie like skin. Not just like a skin-tight suit. She felt naked. And yet not exposed. She could understand now how Hoala never seemed in the least bit shy about shedding her long flowing garment and leaping into the air covered only by her green skin. Hoala wasn't made of skin. Hoala—as hard as this was for Marnie to process along with everything else in the moment—was made of light. She was more alien than Marnie realized. Not in the least bit human at all.

Marnie could feel the difference the wings made. When she glided, she glided much faster and more smoothly. When she pumped her arms, it was like wearing fins in the swimming pool instead of just trying to kick with her measly feet.

Faster, higher, stronger. This suit was an improvement in every way. If only she could show it to Major Zimholt. See if he could design something just like it.

It is yours, she heard Hoala say.

And then Hoala was with her, a quarter-sized dot on Marnie's right hand. Glowing a soft gold. Weightless on Marnie's skin. But real. She was there. Marnie could see her.

The dot of light moved off Marnie's hand, into the air beside her. It grew. Expanded. Changed shape.

Back into the shape of a human with long silvery hair and wide silvery eyes. Wearing green skin and webbing and wings. Looking like Marnie from the neck down. Her own face—although Marnie realized now that that was part of Hoala's suit, too—but otherwise Marnie's twin.

You can see me now, Hoala said.

It was obvious, but Marnie still agreed with her out loud. "Yes."

If I told you the suit gives you the power to make a shelter—

Marnie didn't want to doubt it. She knew it was probably a trick, a way for Hoala to bypass her disbelief, but right now, Marnie was in the mood for miracles. She was in the mood for believing her eyes.

Hoala pointed to a nearby cliff. Marnie's heart was already speeding in anticipation.

Don't think, don't think. Marnie tried to clear her head.

Hoala reached out her right hand and created a platform where she could land.

Marnie closed her eyes. Opened them again. *See it. Believe.*

Her webbed fingers traced a line through the air. Her webbed feet followed, reaching for a place to stand.

It was flimsy. Not exactly up to code. Marnie had to laugh at herself. She was a beginner. But she had done it.

It could be done. She was standing gingerly on top of the proof.

Again, Hoala said.

For a moment, just a brief one, Marnie wished her teacher would just do it for her. But that wasn't the way. That wasn't how to learn. Marnie aimed her webbed hand downward and thought of making something more solid, not so rickety, and it came. Still not as solid as any of the platforms Hoala had ever made, but still better than before.

And better than nothing, which was all Marnie had ever produced before this moment.

She grinned at Hoala. Hoala smiled back. Her liquid silver eyes seemed to sparkle in the sunlight.

Hoala raised her arms. Her wings accordioned outward from her ribs. She built the pyramid around her. Marnie could see her clearly inside it.

Marnie raised her own winged arms. Still feeling a little shaky while she did it. What if it wasn't true? What if it didn't work?

But she had already seen too much in the last half hour to doubt what might happen next.

A thin, too-thin, membrane rose around Marnie's body. It flapped in the wind like a loose, transparent tarp. But Marnie kept on. She anchored it at the top by bringing her hands flat together, the way she had seen Hoala do so many times. The structure was complete, even if it might break apart in the next gust of wind.

"I know," Marnie said before Hoala could. "Do better."

She took a breath. Closed her eyes and opened them. Concentrated on quieting her heart and mind.

Then she traced the same lines, from the base of the platform, outward to her sides, up above her head to join the walls seamlessly together.

A gust blew. The structure held. Again, not nearly as perfect of a hideaway as anything Hoala made, but it was something. It was hers. Marnie had really made it.

She stood side by side with Hoala, both of them encased in their own private shelters. Hoala smiled with approval. Marnie drank it in.

Then Hoala waved away her own walls with a stroke of her hand. She leapt back into the air.

Marnie hated to leave the fort she had built, but she felt almost certain she could build one again. She knew what it felt like now. She knew the pattern.

Marnie waved her hand the way Hoala did. The walls and platform disappeared, just the way she wanted. It really worked. All of it suddenly worked. Marnie wasn't taking any of it for granted.

She leapt from the cliff and spread her winged arms and followed Hoala at a closer distance than she had ever managed before.

Two pale green birds gliding on currents of air.

Not visible to anyone who didn't know how to see them.

Hoala was still more graceful than Marnie, more elegant, faster, smoother, better—but Marnie could see that pattern now, too. It would just take practice, learning how to fly in the new flight suit, learning how to use the webbed fingers and toes and wings.

Can I show this to Major Zimholt? Marnie asked. *So he can make more suits like this?*

Hoala didn't answer right away. Marnie worried she might have gone too far. Maybe she offended Hoala by even asking. It was her technology, after all. A design created by her own alien race, or maybe even by Hoala herself. What right did Marnie have to show it to another human? It was incredibly generous that Hoala had even shared it with her.

There is a reason, Hoala finally answered. *I have to tell you no. I am not permitted to make myself known to him. I hope you will continue to hold my secret.*

Marnie's cheeks burned with embarrassment. *Of course I will hold your secret,* she thought to Hoala. *I will never tell anyone about you.*

And she hadn't, over these past several months. Marnie knew what it was to try to hide. She had to flee so many times because people discovered what she could do.

You can trust me, she assured Hoala.

Hoala turned in the air. She flew back toward Marnie. And then she did something she had never done before.

There, right in midair, she extended her arms out to her sides, quickly this time since there was no place to rest—not yet—and created a bubble around them. A shelter. A hideaway.

It floated. Like an aircraft or a spaceship. And Marnie assumed they were invisible within in, just like when Hoala built her stationary structures.

"I will teach you many things," Hoala said. "I will share with you. I want to help you. I have been waiting for you, Marnie. For many years."

Marnie stared at her, too surprised and too emotional to answer.

Hoala had been waiting for her? How? Why? In what possible world would someone like Hoala care at all that someone like Marnie even existed? Marnie was no one. Even with her strange condition to rule her life, Marnie herself was nothing special. Anyone could pass her on the street and never notice her. She had depended on that anonymity to help hide for the past almost twelve years.

Marnie's voice shook. "I … I don't know what to say."

Hoala clasped Marnie's wrist with her webbed fingers. When Hoala smiled, her wide liquid silver eyes seemed to shine with a special light. They looked as if they were wet with tears, although Marnie never saw a drop of liquid fall.

Marnie's own eyes felt misty. She wasn't used to anyone's attention. Toward the end, even her own mother had forgotten Marnie existed. Or maybe not that she existed—she still used Marnie to carry out her own compulsion—but she stopped caring that Marnie was her daughter, her teenage daughter who still needed love and a mother and a safe and normal life.

"I will teach you many things," Hoala said, "that are for your future. And the future of your species. But first you had to learn to see." Hoala waved her hand. The bubble around them popped. The air rushed in, whipping Marnie's hair into her face, drying the mist in her eyes.

Hoala fell away from her, down toward the crowns of the evergreen forest, down toward the ribbon of stream cutting across the meadows and feeding the flowers crowded all along its banks.

The alien spread her arms wide and rode on the waves of wind. Marnie raced down to catch her, to join her, to follow wherever she flew.

For her life now and for a future she couldn't see yet.

But maybe Hoala could teach her to see that, too.

THE RETURN

1

Sharman Hix batted away another persistent mosquito. Or maybe it was the same one. Buzzing around her nose, distracting her.

She usually covered herself in bug spray all summer long, but she ran out of it yesterday and forgot to pick up more from the supply room at the Factory. Now she was paying for it. Dammit.

Aside from the bugs, Sharman loved the summers up here in the Wasatch Mountain Range outside Salt Lake City, Utah. She grew up in the brown, dry desert of Phoenix, Arizona. The colors of a mountain summer were always a feast for her eyes. The lush green grass, flowers everywhere showing off their yellows and purples and reds, aspens with their rounded green leaves quaking in the breeze—even after six years of living here, she couldn't imagine taking it for granted. Couldn't imagine waking to another summer morning and thinking, *Oh, this again? Whatever.*

Plus the temperatures here were so much more humane. Sometimes it was cool enough in the evenings that she had to throw on a light jacket. Whereas summers in Phoenix, night and day, always used to feel like she was living inside a roaster.

Winter was another matter. Sharman didn't much care for that. Her blood had still never adjusted to the deep cold. But winter was behind her now again, and she intended to enjoy every day until the snows returned in late October.

Enjoy everything except the mosquitos. She swatted the one buzzing around her nose. One down, a million to go.

Sharman focused again on her pilots. She liked to watch the trainees from this cliff while they practiced their maneuvers through the canyon, rather than flying in her own pod out there alongside them. She preferred this vantage point so she could see them all in a group at once.

There were three new pilots this time, and Sharman was only sure about two of them. The third was some hotshot transfer over from the Navy. He thought he was all that and a hundred percent more. Sharman didn't like the guy.

But *like* wasn't the criterion. Could Brett Baston fly? Yes. Very well. Even though he had a harder touch on the pod than Sharman liked to see. She'd have to caution him about that again.

The canyon where they were training had a nice deep drop down to a meandering stream at the bottom, and high vertical cliffs on both sides. Perfect for practicing precision moves with the pods, seeing how they responded to the pilots' instructions to move up, down, and sideways.

The three pods looked like gray bubbles swimming back and forth through the air. Their lower halves were dark gray, and the uppers were transparent, allowing the pilots a full three-sixty view.

The pods were invisible to any outsiders, thanks to whatever the high-tech material was that coated the outside of the spheres. Sharman could see the crafts because she wore a special snug-fitting flight suit made of that same material. Like recognized like. But any random plane flying past or any hiker or paraglider playing nearby wouldn't have a clue what was going on in the airspace in front of them. The pods simply wouldn't exist.

Their invisibility wasn't the only thing special about the pods. They were unlike anything Sharman had ever flown before she came here to work at the Factory. There were no controls inside the pods. Nothing to steer with, nothing to adjust speed or altitude or to make the pod level off if you didn't like its angle.

These were experimental craft. Highly advanced. Of unknown origin, although Sharman still hoped that her boss, Major Fritz Zimholt, would tell her the whole background on them some day.

Sharman had her suspicions. She had heard rumors during the six years she'd been here at the Factory that a lot of the unusual tech came from reverse-engineering ships that might have come in with extraterrestrial pilots.

Did she believe it? Maybe. The universe was a strange place. She had seen things she never read about in school or heard from her parents or teachers.

Sharman had planned to go to a prestigious east coast college after graduating early from high school. She was already a pilot, thanks to a special charity program offered at her school from the time she was eleven.

She was the best pilot in the program. Her instructors never tried to hide that. They told her she could do big things. She should shoot for being an astronaut some day.

That was the plan. Rigorous college courses, physics, chemical engineering—Sharman had laid out a perfect path.

And then came the call from Major Zimholt. Even

though he was already an old man—somewhere in his seventies—he was only a major. Not a colonel or even a general.

But Sharman heard from a guy at the Factory that the major quit the service to come take over his father's manufacturing business. And since the business at the Factory included supplying the military with all sorts of cutting-edge aircraft, it all worked out. Everybody was friends.

She still remembered the exact date of when Major Zimholt called her with an offer. December twenty-first, right after Sharman graduated and just a few days before Christmas.

Forget college, he told her. We can teach you whatever you need to know. Come fly my secret aircraft. Come be the pilot you want to be.

Sharman had a feeling. More than an intellectual or logical decision. It just seemed … right. It all seemed possible, what Major Zimholt said. That she could pilot a spacecraft some day. That she could go flying out through the stars.

She had packed her bags and come over to the Factory when she was eighteen. She was twenty-four now. Time flew, and so did Sharman. Every single day. Exactly what Major Zimholt promised, and exactly what Sharman wanted.

She was the senior pilot at the Factory now, in

charge of training all the others. But that was another problem with Navy flyboy: he treated her like she was a kid. Like she didn't know as much as he did because he had been flying so much longer than she had.

Sharman had no time for that.

"Not flying *these*," she told Baston. The pods were as different from a Navy jet as could be.

The pods were alive. They could think. They had opinions about what they wanted to do.

They were like riding horses, Sharman always told her pilots. You'd better treat them well or they're going to throw you.

Instead of operating the pods with controls, the pilots wore the same kind of special flight suit that Sharman did. It fit them like second skins. They pulled the hoods up over their heads and snugged them to the edge of their cheeks so they were encased in the material from the tops of their heads to their ankles. Over their feet they wore special supple boots made out of the same material.

Sharman always preferred to pilot her pod barefoot. She liked having a skin-to-skin connection with her craft.

In addition to the flight suits, the pilots wore special lighted circlets around their skulls. They were head harnesses that allowed the pods to hear what the pilots were thinking.

Sharman wore a head harness of her own while she

watched the other pilots. It allowed her to hear what was going on between the trainees and their pods.

She had had to rescue more than a few of them over the years by taking control over pods that weren't listening to their particular pilots.

Training wheels, Sharman told the newcomers. She might not like all of the pilots Major Zimholt asked her to train, but she had no desire to see any of them killed.

Any *more* of them killed. There had been too many already. Pilots who had underestimated the power of their craft, or had lost their connection to the pods, or who had simply washed out and given up as the pods raced into the mountainside and crashed.

The two female trainees were doing all right. Nancy Chow had come over from the Air Force and had a nice light touch her pod responded to well. Frieda Wiles was a Navy pilot like Baston, but she wasn't trying to hotshot it the way he was. She was calm and methodical and steady. Like a cowgirl who knew how to ride her horse.

Sharman could see from the way they were flying that both of them took to heart her instructions about respecting their pods' opinions. There should be a give and take. Pilots should make requests, not demands. But not in a wimpy way. Confident, *let's go to the right. That's it. Now up and to the left.*

Pilots had to build trust with their sentient pods. They had to form an actual relationship. Some of the new pilots got that, some never did. And Major Zimholt gave Sharman full authority to say which pilots could stay and which had to go.

Right now she was feeling that Baston would be packing his bags this afternoon. But she didn't want to boot him just because she didn't like his personality. That was juvenile. She was willing to let him try one more time to impress her. But this morning's trial maneuvers were his last chance. She couldn't afford to waste anymore time on a pilot she couldn't teach.

And right now she could see that Baston was still trying to brute his pod around. The craft didn't like it. Sharman didn't blame it. No one liked being manhandled.

"Hey, Baston," she said out loud. Her own head harness would transmit it to Baston's, making it sound like Sharman was talking to him from right inside his pod.

The other two pilots would be able to hear her, too. Sharman was mindful of that. She was never interested in shaming people. She just wanted the pilots to treat her pods right.

"Ease up," she told him. "I can see how tight you are from here." Baston was still trying to control the pod's direction by shifting his body weight left and right. What he needed to do was stop moving at all and just relax his mind and think to the pod what he wanted.

It was like watching a gamer flail around behind the

control as if that might have any effect on what they saw on the screen.

"You just need to think it," Sharman reminded him. "Take a few breaths. Try again. You can do this."

Baston cursed. He knocked his right fist against the inside of the dome.

"Yeah, that's it," Sharman snapped at him. She made no effort to hide her irritation. "Come on back. You're done."

"I can get it!" he argued.

"Not in my pod, you're not. You ever touch one of them like that again, I'll personally kick your ass."

She could hear Baston scoff. It probably seemed like an empty threat. Sharman was five-two, the size of a pixie, and that Baston guy was at the top range of the height Major Zimholt's pilot program allowed. The pods were small and could feel claustrophobic from inside. Anyone over five-foot-seven sat there with their heads half-cocked against the inside of the lid. They filled up the space like someone had crammed them into a hole.

Although … Sharman had reason to believe that didn't have to be true. But she wasn't going to tell Navy boy about that.

She had told Major Zimholt about the anomaly, but it had corrected itself after the event and never happened again.

Sharman was in need of a larger craft one day to transport a passenger, Marnie Stemple. Marnie had been flying after Sharman to try to rescue her from a runaway pod. Flying as in flapping her arms like some kind of human bird.

But the whole thing had gotten so out of hand, by the time Marnie caught up her, she was beyond exhaustion.

Sharman wished she had a way of fitting another person into her pod. She didn't know how she was going to get Marnie back to the Factory safely otherwise.

The pod reacted to that thought. It grew a whole section behind the pilot's seat, big enough for Marnie to climb inside and lie down and pass out.

When the two of them returned to the Factory and climbed out inside the hangar, Sharman's pod melded back into its original configuration.

Sharman had already contacted Major Zimholt to tell him to meet her in the hangar and come look. But even though he came quickly to see it, it was already too late.

After transport came to take Marnie back to her room, Sharman remained in the hangar with Major Zimholt and tried to tell him everything the pod had done.

From flying away with her to a destination of its own, to taking Sharman up higher than she ever imagined the pods could go.

They were there so the pod could show her a spaceship moving through the sky in a place where no space-ship could possibly belong.

And then the expansion of its rearward capacity. Sharman and Major Zimholt stood in front of her pod for a long time analyzing what it all meant.

"Has that ever happened before?" Sharman asked. "Any of it?"

"None of it," Major Zimholt confirmed.

Since that January experience, seven months ago, the two of them had done other trials to see if they could duplicate at least the expansion of any of the pods.

Major Zimholt was a tall man, well above the limit of five-foot-seven. They wondered what a pod would do if he asked it to accommodate his height first before trying to fit inside it.

Would the pod respond the way Sharman's had, and expand to meet the need?

But no matter how many pods they tried it in, including Sharman's own, the craft remained its same petite sphere. Major Zimholt's lanky legs had no chance of folding up inside it.

But Sharman still thought it was a possibility. If it had happened once, it could happen again.

Maybe it just took the right pilot to come along, and a pod would want to grow a little larger to welcome that pilot inside.

Sharman had a lot of theories about the pods. A *lot*. Major Zimholt depended on her and the other pilots to find out how much the pods could actually do. It was why she woke up every day still excited to get out in the air and try. She was an explorer, a test pilot. And she had big plans for the future. Not just flying pods all her life, but graduating to flying a spaceship some day.

But for now she was still building a crew of the best pilots she could find for the Factory.

And Baston wasn't one of them. That flyboy needed to go.

"I said, you're *done,*" Sharman had to repeat from the edge of the cliff. Baston was still trying to wrestle with his pod, not by hitting it this time, but by shouting out mental commands that Sharman could hear inside her own mind. They were giving her a headache.

And then the pod did what Sharman had seen other pods do.

"NO!" she shouted to it. She reached out into the air as if she might be able to grab it and keep it from spinning.

But the pod was out there flying, and Sharman was nowhere near it.

It was like a horse bolting and galloping without any sense of where it was going. Crashing through branches, leaping over fences, just running and running to get away.

Baston had spooked his pod. It wasn't acting this way because it was mad. It was out of control because Baston didn't understand how to just sit inside it and let it do the work.

He must have kicked it or hit it or done something else that Sharman didn't see. The pods needed a steady hand, but it also had to be gentle.

"BASTON!" she called, but he couldn't hear her anymore. The pod was in a full spiral, spinning like a top. He wouldn't know which was was up, he wouldn't be able to think anymore. His brain was spinning too fast to try to regain control.

Sharman watched in horror as the pod spun toward the mountainside.

She had seen this before. Over and over too many times.

"NO!" she shouted again, and she reached out both arms, as though she might catch the pod like a beach ball, just snatch it out of the air.

"Come on, baby!" she told the pod. She had maybe ten more seconds before it crashed, maybe less.

She heard Brett Baston scream. She could picture him with his arms in front of his face, trying to ward off the crash, knowing full well that he couldn't.

Sharman gave it one last desperate effort. She begged the pod to stop.

And then the pod ... bounced. It struck the side of the rocky mountain and bounced right off.

It careened back into the open air, and at half of its previous wild spin.

The pod seemed to lope along as if it was stunned. It floated through the air with a strange jerking motion. Half-halt, half-halt, and then it found a smooth glide again.

Sharman's heart was beating so fast she could barely breathe. She could barely speak.

"B-Bas—?" It was the best she could do.

She could hear his breath heaving. The gasps of a terrified man. Finally Baston managed a weak and shaky, "Yeah."

"You're …" Sharman steadied her own breath. "Okay, so you're all right. Everything is good?"

"Get me down," Baston said feebly. "This thing is out of its mind."

Sharman spoke calmly to the pod inside her mind. She told it it had done a great job, everything was fine.

Baston tried to interrupt her, probably to argue the opposite of everything she was saying, but Sharman was having none of it. She was done with this guy.

"You shut your mouth," she told him. "Shut it right now. Don't think any thoughts. You just be a blank page."

The other two pilots were hovering near. Sharman could feel how shaken both of them were.

"Everybody," she told them, "come on home."

She continued coaxing Baston's pod to return to the flat spot up near her on the cliff where they had all taken off from not long ago.

The two women came back first. Nancy and Frieda popped their dome lids and came out to stand on the dark green grass while Sharman continued to do what she could.

Finally she brought Baston's pod back, too. He barely waited for it to settle onto the ground before he bullied open the lid and came charging out.

He cursed at Sharman. He cursed at the pod. For a minute Sharman thought he might kick it, and then she'd have to shove him off the cliff.

But she saw the red raw look in his eyes. Like he wanted to cry, but he didn't want to do it in front of her or the other two women.

"Dismissed," Sharman said quietly. She didn't want to raise her voice. She felt completely drained. It had been a hell of a morning.

Baston didn't wait to be told again. He stalked off toward the trail. It would be a long hike out, but he probably preferred it to taking the short ride back to the Factory inside the pod.

Sharman sat herself down on the grass. Another damn mosquito took advantage and buzzed around her sweating face.

"You okay?" Nancy Chow asked.

Sharman gave her a thumbs up. Frieda Wiles plopped down beside her own open pod and expressed in colorful terms what an absolute ass Baston was.

"He's lucky you saved him," Frieda said.

"I don't think I did anything," Sharman said. "I tried, but…"

Frieda and Nancy exchanged a look.

"No, we saw you," Nancy said. "Although I still don't get how that worked." She shrugged. "But maybe you'll teach us later."

"Not today, though," Sharman said, standing up slowly on shaky legs. "I think we've all had enough fun."

Sharman still hadn't recovered from the experience, but she needed to be the leader again. She didn't have the luxury of wallowing here in a stupor.

"I'll follow you in a minute," she told the pilots. "You go on back." Sharman's pod was waiting in the shade of a fir tree a short distance away.

Nancy and Frieda got back in their pods and took off at a cruising speed back toward the Factory.

Sharman walked to the edge of the cliff and looked out over the canyon for a few minutes more. As her heartbeat finally found its normal rhythm again, she replayed in her mind everything she had just witnessed.

Sharman had never—*ever*—seen someone survive a pod that was as out of control as Baston's was.

What had he done to make the pod bounce off the mountainside like that? How was it possible? The pods weren't made that way.

He's lucky you saved him. We saw you.

Could Nancy Chow be right? Was it possible Sharman really did have something to do with how the pod reacted? She remembered reaching out her arms to it, picturing it like a giant beach ball. Could her panicked thought actually have made the pod bounce like that?

There was a sound of footsteps on dirt behind her. Someone coming up from the trail.

Baston must have cooled off by now and realized he was a fool to hike out on foot when he had a pod sitting up here that he could pilot back to the Factory in just a few minutes.

Pilot it slowly, sure. But maybe the guy was brave enough to get back on the horse that threw him. Points to flyboy for having some nerve.

Sharman turned to greet him.

But it wasn't Brett Baston coming toward her from the top of the trail.

It was a black man, as black as Sharman, with a thick head of gray hair. He looked like he might be in his seventies. Maybe older. Sharman had a hard time judging people's ages.

"Can I help you, sir?" she asked. Maybe he was a lost hiker. He was dressed like one in loose cargo pants made out of some technical fabric and a tan T-shirt that showed a surprisingly strong build. The old man looked fit.

Sharman never saw strangers out here this far. But she wasn't worried about her safety. The man was old. Even though she was smaller, she figured she could take him. And besides, he stayed at a respectful distance, maybe to show her he was harmless.

And her pod was right there. She could reach it in just a few steps. Hop right in and take off if she needed to. The man would wonder where she went when she just disappeared inside the invisible craft, but maybe he'd put it down to some side effect from his medication. If Sharman needed to leave, she would leave.

The old man smiled at her. "So you're twenty-four now?" he said.

His statement didn't compute. "Excuse me?"

"Sharman Hix," the man said. "Twenty-four. Turning twenty-five on August tenth."

Sharman didn't like this at all. "Do I know you?" It was a rhetorical question. She knew very well she had never met this man. Her nerves were buzzing. She was on high alert. This was one too many weird things to happen on an already overloaded morning.

The man took another step toward her. Sharman held her ground. She had nowhere to go but over the side of the cliff, and unlike Marnie Stemple, she couldn't just flap her arms and fly.

"I'm Reginald Swan," the man said. "Reggie. We haven't met yet, but we will."

Sharman looked at him like the crazy man he obviously was. It was time to go. She didn't have to listen to this.

"You wonder why it bounced," said Reginald Swan.

Sharman's face went slack. She nodded. And quickly tried to reassess.

"I'm sorry, sir, *who* are you?"

And then someone from the Factory flew in on a pod.

The pilot circled once above Sharman and the old man, then set the pod down on the grass between them.

The lid popped open and the pilot got out.

The pilot was Sharman Hix.

2

Sharman stared at the woman standing on the grass in her matte gray flight suit and her bare feet.

She looked older than Sharman, maybe by ten or fifteen years. Sharman was a terrible judge of ages.

Older Sharman pushed back the hood on her flight suit, revealing hair she kept cropped short, just like Sharman did now. But there were a few gray hairs in there. Sharman wondered when she started getting those.

Her older self looked more filled out than Sharman, maybe by about ten pounds. But it looked good on her. She was a full-grown adult. Not some twenty-four-year-old pixie who headed up the pilot program.

"Take it in," the older Sharman said.

"I am. I have."

"Good," her older self said. "Got anything to eat?"

It was such a normal and yet bizarre question, Sharman laughed. Of course any version of her would be hungry right now. Sharman was starving, too.

She had brought a few snacks in a pint-sized pack that she stowed under her feet inside her pod. She pointed to the pod now. Older Sharman headed right over without hesitation.

"We left in a hurry," Reginald Swan said. "Got the pods from Fritz and came right over."

The light dawned in Sharman's mind.

"So … did you guys save Baston?"

Older Sharman tore into the wrapper on a chocolate and almond energy bar. Then she took a swig of the small bottle of water, and offered it to Sharman.

Sharman declined. She was thirsty, but she didn't want to deprive her grown woman self of the drink if she needed it.

And she didn't have any extra for Mr. Swan. She was feeling bad about that.

But he dug into the cargo pocket at the side of his right thigh and pulled out a bag of trail mix. No water, but if he didn't bring it, that wasn't really Sharman's problem.

"Here." Older Sharman came to where Sharman still stood with her back to the open canyon. The older woman had eaten only half of the chocolate and almond bar and drank only half of the water.

Sharman took both and thanked her. Then she shook her head. This was all too weird.

"Take a seat," her older self said. "Reggie can explain about the bounce. He taught me." Older Sharman smiled. "Today, in fact. Just like this. Welcome to our life, little Sharman. Trust me, it gets even weirder."

Sharman liked that her grown self could joke around with her like this. And she didn't mind being called *little Sharman,* even though she would have hated it from anyone else.

"What do I call you?" she asked her older self as the two of them settled cross-legged on the grass. The way older Sharman did it was exactly like Sharman did. Same same. Same face, same way of talking, same physical gestures, everything.

Mr. Swan chuckled. "Commander would be nice."

"Commander?" Sharman repeated. She looked at her older self with awe.

So she really did do it. They did it.

"Commander of a spaceship?" she asked, just to make sure.

Older Sharman raised her eyebrows and gave a nod.

Sharman smiled and gave the same nod back.

Hot damn. They did it.

"But friends call me Shar now," the older one said. "As if Sharman's too big a mouthful."

"I'm afraid we're on a short timeline," said Mr. Swan. "Commander's got actual commanding to do."

"So you're … on the ship, too?" Sharman asked.

"No, he's sticking around for a while," Shar said. "I'm the one who has to take off."

Sharman handed her back the last little bit of water in her bottle. A commander should get the last drink. Sharman could get plenty later.

She felt suddenly young and small and shy. Like a little sister to this impressive woman. Like a different person, not an earlier version of the commander she always hoped to be.

But Shar thanked her for the water and quickly swigged it down. Then she leaned back on her open palms and turned her attention to Reginald Swan.

"Tell her like you told me," Shar said.

"Don't think it could be any other way," he said. "Do you?"

"Reggie designed these pods," Shar said. "He taught Fritz Zimholt how to make them."

"I could make them," Reginald said, "but it didn't mean I understood them."

"But how?" Sharman asked. "I don't get that."

"I learned it from three friends of mine," Reginald said. "Called them RayJay, Linus, and Mit. But those weren't their real names. I couldn't pronounce their real names—still can't. My friends were extraterrestrials."

Sharman saw her older self check her reaction. But Sharman took it in. She wasn't shocked by the news. She'd been hearing rumors for several years.

"They taught me how to make them," Reginald said. "And they taught me some of how to fly them. But they had to leave and go back home before they could teach it all to me." He paused and ate the last of his trail mix. "But I went to their planet and found them again. And I stayed a good long time and learned all the rest."

"You went," Sharman said. "To another planet."

She traded a glance with her older self. Commander Shar was clearly enjoying the exchange. She must have remembered how she felt the first time she heard it.

"Talk about the bounce," Shar said. She wasn't wearing a watch, but Sharman knew her older self was keeping track of the time. Sharman did it, too, guessing throughout the day what time it was, then checking to see if she was right.

There were no clocks inside the pods. Sharman tried to teach the pilots to judge on their own how long they were out flying. She also taught them to estimate distances. Sharman was always working on that herself. But older Sharman must be a master of all that by now.

"Have you ever had a real, honest, maybe even spooky connection with your pod? Maybe you even felt that you *were* the pod?"

"Yes," Sharman said eagerly. "I did. Just once, last January."

"When it took you to the ship," older Sharman said.

"Yes," Sharman answered. "Exactly."

Of course her older self would have all the same

memories. But it still made Sharman happy to hear that Shar knew what she was talking about.

"It's hard to describe," Sharman told Reginald. "But … I was it. It was me. I wasn't just riding inside it, I *was* it. So yeah, I know what you're saying."

"That's the gold standard," Reginald said. "That's how you should be feeling all the time. But I didn't get that. I thought we were just supposed to talk to the pods with our minds. Like they were separate from us. But they're not."

Older Sharman groaned good-naturedly. "Tell her about the bounce!"

"You have these flight suits," Reginald said. "They're like a second skin."

Sharman nodded. She knew that. She was starting to feel as impatient as her older self.

"Well, the pods are a third skin," Reginald said. "They're still you. You're wearing them. You are them." He shook his head. "I still don't know how to explain this right." He lifted his chin at Shar. "You say it."

She laughed. "I know it now, but I didn't know it when you told me. Keep it the same. Let's not alter time. You're going to have to keep going."

Sharman felt a slight swoon in her mind. This was all real. This was time travel. Her older self was keeping it honest. *Right and tight,* as one of Sharman's old flight instructors liked to say.

Reginald Swan slapped at a mosquito trying to sample his arm.

"But fast," older Sharman told him. "I need to still be here when you finish."

"Here's another thing I didn't get," Reginald said. "Until I saw RayJay and the guys back on their planet. I think they didn't want to tell me while we were all still living on the base. They didn't want to give out that much information to our military."

He smiled at Sharman with what looked like a mixture of both mischief and pride, like a magician about to reveal his trick. "The power source for the pods. Have you guessed yet what it is?"

"Some kind of … alien technology?" It seemed obvious now that they were talking about aliens out loud.

Reginald pointed at Sharman. "It's you." Then he pointed at himself and the older Sharman. "It's me. It's her. It's whoever is flying the pod. It draws its energy from the living pilot. That's why I said it's like a third skin. It's only flying around because there's something alive inside it."

"Wait," Sharman said. She had to process the information. But one glance at her older self told her she'd better keep going now and process it all later.

"Why do you have to leave?" she asked Shar.

Older Sharman blew out a breath. "If you only knew." She reached over and clasped Sharman's shoulder. "You'll get it when it's your turn, but I'm sorry, I can't tell you more than that." Then she motioned for Reginald Swan to hurry up.

He didn't seem offended. In fact, the two of them seemed like good friends. He must be used to Sharman treating him so casually, even though he was so much older than she was.

"You work too hard," he told Sharman. "We all did. We thought we had to work so hard to control the pods. But you'll figure it out from here now. How to just relax and put it on like an outer coat. Then you save the real work for when you need to power up a force field around the pod."

"A force field?"

"There," older Sharman said with satisfaction. "Finally, about the bounce."

"Shar here flew her pod nice and close to Baston's," Reginald said. "She spent some energy creating a force field. If you're close, you can extend it to somebody else."

"Oh," Sharman said. "*OH.* So that's what Nancy meant? She said I saved Baston. Does that mean she saw you?"

"Couldn't help it," Shar said. "But I knew you didn't see me. Because *I* didn't see me, back when I was you."

"So you flew in—"

"And she wrapped him in her force field," Reginald

said. "No crash. Just a bounce. You'll try it now, you'll find out."

Older Sharman abruptly rose to her feet. "That's it, gang. Gotta go."

She brushed the grass and dirt from the back of her flight suit, then she held out her arms to give Sharman a hug.

"I'm so proud of you," older Sharman said. "You have no idea. You are so kickass, girl. Just keep it up. You're the reason for everything I get to do."

Sharman hugged her back hard. It was the strangest sensation. But she was back to thinking of her older self like a big sister who had come to visit.

Reginald Swan rose, too, and gave older Sharman a friendly hug.

"See you when I see you," he said.

"Yep," older Sharman answered. She was busy tucking loose strands of hair back under the hood of her flight suit. Then she climbed into her pod.

"Is your ship here?" Sharman asked her.

"Not far," Shar said. She pointed straight up.

"So are you flying the pod back to it?"

Older Sharman scoffed. "This thing? I've got my own stashed near the Factory."

"She couldn't fly it here," Reginald explained. "It would draw too much attention."

Sharman nodded. She got it. If Nancy or Frieda had seen some strange, upgraded craft come flying in, they would have realized someone else, not Sharman, had saved Baston.

Why that mattered, Sharman wasn't sure. But she knew there wasn't time now to ask any more questions.

"Keep up the good work," older Sharman said. "Seriously." Then with a last smile for her younger self, she closed the lid on her pod and raced off into the sky.

Sharman watched her go for as long as she could. Finally the gray bubble was out of sight.

She turned to Mr. Swan. "But you're really staying?"

"For a while."

"Because of … me?" she asked shyly. Now that the two of them were alone again, she felt like she needed to treat him more formally. He might be friends with her older self, but he was still a stranger to her.

"Fritz Zimholt is an old friend," Reginald said.

"Oh," Sharman said quickly. "Of course." She should have realized that when she found out Mr. Swan had designed the pods and taught Major Zimholt how to build them.

"And yes," Reginald added, "because of you. There are some things I can teach you, if you want to know them."

"Yes!" Sharman said. "Are you kidding? I want to know everything!"

Reginald Swan chuckled.

"Did you … did you teach her?" Sharman asked. "You know—me?"

"Is it making your head spin yet?" Reginald asked.

"All this trying to figure out what's future and what's present?"

"Spinning right off my neck," Sharman confessed.

"It'll get easier," Reginald said. "Give it time. I'm not in such a hurry the way you are." He pointed to the sky, the way older Sharman did. "I'll stick around. We'll practice a few things."

Mr. Swan turned back toward the hiking trail. For a moment Sharman thought he might be about to hike back.

But then he did something she didn't even know you could do.

He whistled for his pod.

The craft rose up from wherever he had left it, just beneath the rise of the hill.

"Like that trick," Reginald said with a smile.

Sharman whistled to her own pod. It stayed exactly where it was, in the shade of the fir tree.

"It takes a certain touch," Reginald said. "You'll get it, Commander Hix." Then with a casual salute at his forehead, he left Sharman alone to deal with everything that had happened.

Sharman smiled. *Commander Hix.* Can you believe it. Yes, I can.

But she was still hungry. And she was thirsty. Younger, older, future, present…

It might have been a huge day, but it was still just a

day. And it was going to take a series of days to get her to be the woman she just met.

Sharman Hix went to her pod. She pulled off her set of supple black flight boots and tucked them inside like she always did. She was glad to see her older self still barefoot. It meant that the technique was sound.

Sharman climbed in and spread her bare toes against the inner skin of the pod.

No, *her* skin. Her third skin. She was going to have to figure out exactly what Reginald Swan meant by that.

But she had time. They had time. Her and Mr. Swan and future Sharman.

Sharman asked her pod to take her home. Powered, she knew now, by the energy of her own beating heart.

Next in the Dove Season Universe
MAKER

- A mechanical genius joins a top-secret mission to learn about alien technology from the aliens themselves. What he discovers changes everything.
- A linguist with the unique ability to communicate with anyone—human or otherwise—uncovers the secrets of an alien race.
- At an elite science conference at a remote mountain retreat, a theoretical physicist learns that her theories are closer to reality than she thought. But even her wildest imaginings do not prepare her for the truth.
- What if death is only one possible outcome, and there are ways to continue a life? For a grieving husband, the only choice is to find his wife again.

A standalone collection in the Dove Season Universe. The future is what we make it.

ABOUT THE AUTHOR

Robin Brande is an award-winning author, former trial attorney, black belt in martial arts, Reiki Master, and wilderness medic. Her outdoor adventures range from the Rocky Mountains to the Alps to Iceland.

She writes in multiple genres, including mystery, adventure, fantasy, science fiction, young adult, romance, and self-help.

For more information:
https://robinbrande.com/

For updates about upcoming installments of DOVE SEASON, along with previews and special discounts, subscribe to the Robin Brande newsletter: https:// robinbrande.com/pages/subscribe.

MORE FROM ROBIN BRANDE

SHOW YOUR BOOK-LOVING STYLE!

AND SCIENCE LOVING, ART LOVING, DOG AND CAT LOVING, AND MORE...

Treat yourself to a soft, comfy, custom-made T-shirt designed by Robin Brande herself, inspired by her own books. You can see all of them at robinbrande.com/collections/t-shirts.

And here's a secret just for you: Use the discount code **READER10** at checkout to get **10% off any items in the store**. That means books, T-shirts, hoodies, mugs—whatever you'd like. Go ahead and treat yourself, book lover.

CERTIFIED
BOOK NERD
CERTIFIED
DOG NERD
CERTIFIED
SCIENCE NERD

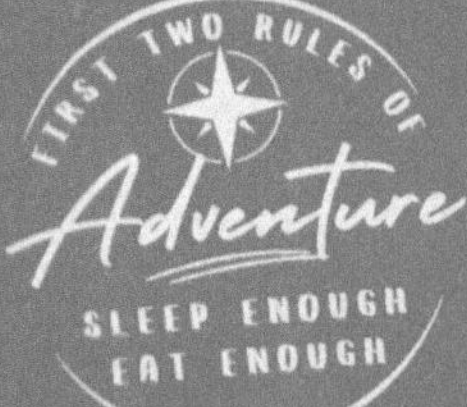
books
every
day
Sleep enough
Eat enough
FIRST TWO RULES OF
Adventure
SLEEP ENOUGH
EAT ENOUGH

Retired psychology professor Dr. Winifred Parsons spent decades studying the human psyche as a scientist and academic. But she also explored it from another angle: Winnie Parsons is clairvoyant.

Now Winnie uses her psi talent to help clients resolve mysteries that are outside the reach of standard investigations.

The path to justice might be twisted, but Winnie always finds a way.

Life after death, miracle healings, communication with other species...

- *The Water Healers*: A nurse investigates rumors of miracle healers in Mexico.
- *A Drop of Sweat*: A clairvoyant secretly uses her skills to unravel the mystery of who destroyed a scientist's lab.
- *The Refugees*: A volunteer helps the refugees fleeing a planetary disaster.
- *The Bridge*: A grieving widow refuses to believe her husband is gone forever.
- *The Outpost Away from the World*: A scientist returns to the off-the-grid cabin of her childhood and discovers the mysterious secret to her survival.

The mountains can dish it out. But that doesn't mean you have to take it.

- *On Red Mountain*: A woman must survive alone in the mountains after her husband is struck by lightning.
- *The Rescue*: A mountain hermit and his dog race to avert a coming disaster—one that the dog senses before anyone else.
- *Home Deer*: A mountain widow takes matters into her own hands to protect the nearby woodland creatures.
- *The Gold Hunter*: An injured climber's only hope for survival is a stranger who won't give up.
- *Taken at Rustler Pass*: A teen girl fights to survive against the stranger who wants her dead.

High school senior and amateur physicist Audie Masters discovers a parallel universe—along with a parallel version of herself.

It's the adventure of a lifetime.

Now all she has to do is survive it.

Read all four books in the exciting, mind-bending PARALLELO-GRAM QUARTET. You'll never look at the universe or your own life the same way again.